# THE LOVE TREE

When Lily arrives at The Limes to work as a maid for two sisters, Eta and Mabel, little does she know she will instantly fall in love with their handsome lodger, Samuel. When Cecil Potts visits the sisters' beer house and shop, a tale of murder, death and deceit unravels. Will Lily and Samuel ever step out from Cecil's dark shadow to find happiness under the love tree?

# PATRICIA KEYSON

◆

# THE LOVE TREE

*Complete and Unabridged*

## LINFORD
*Leicester*

First published in Great Britain in 2020

First Linford Edition
published 2021

A catalogue record for this book is available
from the British Library.

ISBN 978–1–4448–4737–6

Published by
Ulverscroft Limited
Anstey, Leicestershire

Printed and bound in Great Britain by
TJ Books Ltd., Padstow, Cornwall

This book is printed on acid-free paper

# 1

Lily trudged through the snow, trying to keep the hem of her skirt from getting sodden and dirty. She was tired after her journey and was anxious about her arrival at her new employers' house. After arriving in the village, and then turning once more she was sure she was in the correct street as the church was clearly visible. The Limes was opposite. It was a fairly large brick-built house with four windows at the front, two up and two down, with the front door off-centre. She wouldn't use the front door.

Large, soft snowflakes started to fall again and she licked some from her lips before standing at the gate of the church-yard and peering in. Sadness at leaving her mum and family welled inside her. She went into the churchyard and looked at a new grave and saw a simple wooden cross. Whoever it was died in 1893, just a short time ago. The cold made her hurry back through the churchyard gate. Although she was nineteen Lily had never lived away from home before. Nervousness and excitement fought for importance. She took a few deep breaths before moving away from the gate, crossing the lane and walking to the side of the house to find an entrance suitable for a maid.

At the far side was a door which wasn't fully closed. She pushed it open, a bell tinkled, and she saw that it opened into the beer house and shop. She'd been told her duties would include serving there. After stepping inside, she looked around. The shelves displayed a variety of goods and on the wooden floor were open sacks containing flour and tea. A few benches provided seating for anyone wanting to drink beer on the premises.

A tall, upright woman walked in through an inner doorway. 'Good afternoon, how may I help you?'

Lily cleared her throat. 'I'm Lily Harrison, the new maid. I'm here to work for the Misses Stratford.'

2

The woman looked her up and down. 'I am the older Miss Stratford. I hope you will be up to the work. You came recommended by one of our highly thought of customers. It was a pity we were unable to interview you, but the distance was too great and carriages are costly. Follow me and I'll show you the house.'

Lily followed her through the shop and into a room which was decorated in a manner quite different from her simple home and the farmhouse where she had been working.

'The parlour,' Miss Stratford announced. The room was dark and cluttered. There was a mix of colours and patterns and there were numerous paintings, photographs, ornaments and bric-a-brac, including porcelain figures, and wax flowers under a glass dome. The largest picture on the wall above the fireplace was of Queen Victoria. Lily felt sad for her as her husband, Prince Albert, had died a long time ago, even before Lily had been born. A man was sitting at a desk at the window, his back to them.

'Samuel, our new maid, Lily Harrison, is here.'

The man hurriedly pushed his chair back, stood and turned. 'Sorry, Eta,' he addressed the older Miss Stratford, 'I was engrossed. Another poem.' He waved his hand at the desk.

Eta said, 'Mr Parker is our lodger. A family friend too.'

Lily's eyes met his and they both smiled. Her heart did a little flip. He was a very handsome young man.

'Hello, Lily. I hope you will be happy at The Limes. The Misses Stratford will be good to you. It's a happy house.'

'Thank you, Samuel, we like to think so.' Eta relaxed her shoulders and sat in an upright chair, not offering Lily a seat. 'The house belonged to our parents and Father opened the shop and beer house, calling it Stratford's Beer House. We've been accepted now, but some of the villagers thought it unseemly for two women to run the beer house when our parents died several years ago. We employ

4

a woman from the village, Bertha, to work in the shop at times which helps a great deal.' She paused for breath and fiddled with the folds of her dress. 'My sister, Mabel, has a weak constitution and is rather frail. Because of her state of health, we need what money we can get so we can pay for the doctor's bills. As Mabel is unable to do a lot of physical work, we need your help with the shop as well as looking after the house and Mabel.'

Lily gasped, but tried to keep it muted. She'd had no idea she would have quite so much to do, but she would try her best, especially if she would be spending time with the good-looking Samuel. He was tall and striking with a neatly trimmed beard and moustache. His dark brown hair was short enough to reveal dainty ears, but what she was drawn to most of all were his piercingly blue eyes. Her cheeks felt hot as she looked at him and found him staring back at her.

Eta continued, 'Mabel likes to be quiet and doesn't like a lot of people around, especially coarse, vulgar ones, who can sometimes be found in the beer house. I hope you are not as easily offended as she is.'

Lily shook her head. 'I don't take offence.'

'Good. Now I think it's time to take you to meet my sister.'

Immediately, Samuel went to the door and opened it for them.

As Lily trailed upstairs with Eta, she couldn't help wishing she'd been offered a drink or been allowed to change out of her wet clothes first. However, the house seemed welcoming and she thought Miss Stratford would be all right to work for. She hoped the younger sister wouldn't be too ill; her own family were all robust and hardly had a day's illness.

Eta opened a door and Lily followed her into a room which smelt of lavender. 'Mabel, my dear, this is Lily Harrison, the maid we were expecting. She's trudged through the snow to be with us.' Eta smiled at her sister who was lying back on the pillows on the bed. She struggled to get up. 'Now, don't you move, please stay comfortable.'

'Lily Harrison, what a lovely name that is.' Mabel held out a hand to Lily and Eta tutted. 'It's nice to meet you, Lily. Come closer to the fire. Eta makes sure I am warm and cosy, but you look frozen like a snowman.'

The woman on the bed was much smaller and friendlier than her older sister. Even though Lily had only just met her, she thought the younger Miss Stratford was kind. The first thing Lily noted about her appearance were the very thick eyebrows which almost overwhelmed her face. Her nondescript brown hair was fanned on the pillow and there were frown lines on her forehead. Lily tried to think of a kind word for her appearance, but there was none. She was very plain. However, her manner made up for it.

Miss Stratford busied herself plumping up the pillows and tidying her younger sister's room while Lily waited patiently. 'I might as well admit to mothering my sister as you will soon realise that's what

I do,' she said, as she re-arranged items on the dressing table.

Lily thought she seemed less scary than before and tried to relax. The younger Miss Stratford's eyes were closed and Lily noticed the dark circles under them.

Miss Stratford put her fingers to her lips and beckoned her to the door. They both slipped quietly out of the room.

'This is your room.' The door was opened onto a room with heavy, dark furniture, flowery wallpaper, a medley of rugs and a musty smell. Eta walked over to the window and opened the shutters letting in the light. 'I'm afraid Mabel and I haven't had the time or energy to do anything in here since our parents died. It was their room and neither of us wanted it although it's the biggest of the four. The three of us are settled in our rooms and, although not suitable for a maid, it will be comfortable for you.'

Lily gave a shiver. She glanced at the empty grate and wished she had a warm and cosy room like Mabel.

Miss Stratford walked to the door.

'You can have a little time to settle in and unpack your things. Then I need you in the kitchen to prepare our evening meal. I will supervise the preparation until you are able to do it on your own. Samuel takes his meals with Mabel, if she is well enough, and me in the dining room. You will eat in the kitchen when you have finished serving us and clearing up afterwards.

Lily slumped on the bed which made the headboard creak. It was a dismal room. Her family home was simple and plain, but this house was full of furniture, pictures and clutter, making Lily want to gasp for air. It felt uncomfortable and changes had to be made straight away. She moved a couple of chairs and little tables and then put some of the more ornate covers and ornaments in the bottom of the wardrobe, hoping there wouldn't be any trouble with Miss Stratford.

The aspidistra in an ornate pot on one of the tables was looking half dead and the dryness of the soil told her why.

Later, she'd bring water up.

She emptied a couple of drawers by putting the things in other half-empty drawers and started to unpack her bag although there wasn't much in it. Her hope was that clothes would be provided for her to wear when working.

After changing into a dry dress, she decided to go down to the kitchen so checked herself in the cheval mirror. Her wavy, light brown hair was frizzy after getting wet and needed taming into a rough knot on the top of her head, but otherwise her appearance was presentable and neat. In the mirror her tall, slim figure looked attractive and her confidence rose. It was important that this job was successful as her family were relying on the money she would send home to them.

When she went downstairs she easily found the kitchen off the hallway. Miss Stratford was already there and getting vegetables in from the scullery. 'You've got an easy meal to cook tonight. We're having leftover cold meat from yesterday. You need to prepare and cook the vegetables, and make a suet pudding. I should be in the shop now, as Bertha will be rushed off her feet. I'll leave you to it.'

Everything took Lily longer than usual as she had to accustom herself to where things were kept. She was feeling hot and red in the face when Samuel entered the kitchen.

'How are you getting on?' he asked.

'I've got everything cooking now. It's quite difficult when you start in a new place.'

'Where were you before?'

'I worked in a farmhouse, but lived at home. It feels strange to think I won't see my family for quite a while.'

Samuel looked thoughtful. 'I'm sorry for you, but you couldn't have wished for a better position than the one you have here. It will be hard work, but they are kind women, and I'll look out for you.'

'Thank you. And what do you do?' Lily hoped he wouldn't mind her asking.

'I'm an artist and a poet.'

'I've never met either before.' Lily thought it sounded romantic.

11

'What about you? Are you artistic?' he asked.

She giggled. 'No.'

'What do you like to do when you aren't working?'

'I've never had much time, but I do like sewing.'

'There you see, you are artistic.'

As she checked on the vegetables a surge of confidence swept through her. He was a thoughtful man and had made her feel better about herself and her position.

'You'd think a man of twenty-four would be making enough income to keep himself, wouldn't you?' Samuel chuckled. 'I don't make much money from my paintings. My parents left me some money which allows me to pay my rent.'

'I'm sorry to hear they've died. I don't know what I'd do if anything happened to my parents.'

'You'd manage. I think you have an inner strength, Lily. Wait and see. When you need it, you'll find it.'

He was very kind. It would be good

if she could spend time with him here at The Limes, but his next words were discouraging.

'I like it here very much because the Misses Stratford leave me to my own devices. It's solitude I need for my painting and poetry.'

There wasn't much likelihood he'd show any interest in her if he liked to be alone. Nevertheless, she looked forward to finding out more about this interesting and attractive man.

# 2

Lily soon got into a routine of getting up early and going downstairs to begin the cleaning and lighting of the fires before the sisters got up. When she heard them about, she started the breakfast for them and Samuel, wishing she could pile Samuel's plate high, but knowing she dare not. She hummed to herself as she placed ham and eggs into a dish to be taken through to the dining room. Eta always put something in the pantry and Lily could only guess these things came from the shop. So far, she hadn't been asked to make bread as it seemed plentiful. At the farm where she'd worked previously, she'd used the breadmaking skills her mother had taught her.

Her stomach tightened in anticipation of her own breakfast, but she would have to wait. She didn't mind eating in the kitchen, but it would have been nice to have a bit of company and someone

14

to talk to.

'Thank you, Lily, this looks delicious,' said Mabel, when Lily placed the breakfast plates on the sideboard for them to help themselves.

Lily thought Miss Mabel looked extra pale that morning, but it wasn't her place to say anything. Eta just nodded and got up to help herself to food. To Lily's disappointment, there was no sign of Samuel. She returned to the kitchen and carried in the large teapot. By the time it was her turn to have some, it would be cold, or at best, tepid, she thought.

When she heard Miss Stratford and Mabel leave the dining room, Lily cleared the table and sat in the kitchen with a plate of bread and ham in front of her and a cup of tea into which she put two spoonsful of sugar.

'That looks good, is there any left?'

Lily nearly choked on her bread as she leapt up and said, 'Oh, Mr Parker! I didn't expect you to come into the kitchen. I'm sorry, I should have waited, but you weren't in the dining room with the sisters.' She knew she was gabbling and told herself to be quiet.

Samuel smiled. 'You must call me Samuel. I was hoping to eat with you. I've been out painting, catching the early morning light. It's freezing out there. I could do with a hot cup of something.'

'I'll boil some more water, this tea is barely warm,' said Lily, going to the range.

'Thank you. I'll help myself to food, but is there a spare plate somewhere?' He looked around the kitchen helplessly.

Lily reached into a cupboard and found one which she put on the table in front of Samuel, pushing the ham, and bread and butter nearer to him. What a lovely start to the day, she thought. If only she wasn't wearing the uniform Eta had given her. Lily wondered where she'd got it from as she didn't think they'd had a maid before. Perhaps one of the customers had passed it on. It was far too big and, although Lily had done her best at altering it, the fit was not good. The material billowed out around her chest and the sleeves were unshapely. She felt untidy in it and was almost ashamed to be seen wearing it in front of Samuel. It would have been nice to look beautiful and well-dressed so he'd appreciate her.

From then on, Samuel occasionally came into the kitchen to eat with Lily if he'd been out early or if he had risen late. She looked forward to being with him, and hoped he felt the same way. But he was inscrutable and she couldn't tell at all.

Lily's favourite task was attending to Mabel who treated her more as a friend than a maid.

One day, Lily went to Mabel's room and found her still in bed. 'Are you getting up and dressed today?' she asked.

'I suppose I should, but I really don't feel like it. I'd like to stay here for a week.' Then she laughed and wriggled upright, swinging her legs over the side of the bed. 'We'd better keep Eta happy, hadn't we?'

Lily smiled and helped Mabel to get washed and dressed. As she did so, Mabel said, 'I expect you think Eta is a peculiar name for my sister. It's short for

Henrietta. My fault, as I couldn't say her name and Mother and Father thought it funny I called her Eta. I don't think Eta was pleased at the time, but she seems to have got used to it over the years. Don't let her intimidate you, she's got a heart full of love and she cares for me dearly, as I do for her.'

Lily was sure what Mabel said was true, but she still compared the two sisters. Miss Stratford was quite different and kept her distance. Every day at breakfast she told Lily what was required of her, and being used to household tasks they weren't a problem. Serving in the shop and beer house was a different matter. There was no difficulty in stacking shelves and weighing out goods. The problem was some of the customers, particularly a few of the men when they'd had too many beers. Miss Stratford and Bertha both had a knack of dealing with them and they never made lewd comments to either of them, and Mabel seemed to avoid serving as much as possible. Lily hated it when someone touched her or pulled at her arm to get her attention. She consoled herself with the thought that chatting to most people was enjoyable and gave her a picture of life in the village outside The Limes.

One of her best times of the day was the evening when the range was damped down for the night, and the kitchen was tidy. It was then she attended to the basket of mending and altering which was left for her. Sometimes she would have Samuel's socks to mend and she did her best with them. She giggled when she imagined darning them artistically in different coloured yarns. As she darned, she thought of Samuel and reflected it would be nice to spend more time with him. Apart from sometimes taking breakfast with her, he often took himself off to paint, so she didn't see much of him, much to her disappointment. She hadn't seen his paintings as, when she cleaned his room, they were covered with old sheets. Perhaps one day she'd pluck up enough courage to ask to look at them.

Then, taking her by surprise, a few

days later Samuel came into the garden where Lily was enjoying some fresh air and doing a few jobs.

'I'll help you,' he said, coming up behind her and startling her. Lily was pleased to have his company and said she'd welcome a strong hand. Together, they pulled at branches which had been blown from the apple tree and Lily dragged them down the garden for chopping up later for the fires indoors when the wood had seasoned.

When she returned to the tree, Samuel was sitting on the ground by the trunk clutching his arm. Blood was seeping through his shirt and he looked pale. 'That branch came back on me. See that sharp bit.'

There was an angled piece of wood with a pointed end lying a little way off.

'How did that happen?' she asked.

'The branch was broken off, half hanging from the tree and I thought I could break it off completely. It ricocheted. I should have got the saw. Eta would have done.'

Lily knelt beside him. 'The bleeding is quite bad, Samuel, you must come inside and let me dress it.'

'It's nothing,' he protested, making an effort to stand.

'I'm going to have to tell Miss Stratford if you don't come in and let me look at it,' Lily insisted.

Samuel managed a small grin. 'All right, you've convinced me.'

Between them they got to the kitchen and Samuel sat on a chair while Lily boiled some water and put it in a bowl and took a clean cloth from a drawer. What she could use for a bandage, she had no idea. Then her petticoat came to mind. She went into the scullery and raised her skirt, tearing at the material underneath. Returning to the kitchen, she said, 'You'll have to take off your shirt. I hope it hasn't stuck to your arm.'

Samuel eased his shirt over his head and blood flowed freely. Lily didn't see the blood, all she noticed was Samuel's bare chest. She was transfixed and couldn't take her eyes from it. There was not a hair to be seen and his muscles were large and well-developed. All she could think about was being enveloped by his strong arms and being held close to him. She felt faint and wondered if she'd need medical aid herself!

'Are you all right?' asked Samuel, looking at her with concern on his face. 'Is the blood making you feel unwell?'

Lily jerked herself out of her reverie and cleaned the wound. Then she wrapped the strips of her petticoat around his arm and told him he should rest. Not trusting herself to stay close to him for longer, Lily rushed back to the garden.

A week later, Lily was sitting with Mabel one evening listening to her playing the piano. It was calm and restful and Lily was mending a pillowslip while she enjoyed the music. No one in Lily's family had any interest in music, so this was a new experience for her. From time to time she watched Mabel's fingers glide over the keys. Mabel didn't always need a score from which to play, she could memorise the tunes.

When the music finished, Lily said, 'That was beautiful, Miss Mabel. You play well.'

'Perhaps, but it's nothing compared with what you do. Your sewing is exquisite and it's a useful gift. Mine is of no use at all.'

'But it gives pleasure to people.'

Mabel closed the piano lid. 'Mother and Father used to like to listen to me playing.' She lowered her voice. 'Eta wasn't good at music, she was more interested in what I'll call masculine things like gardening and woodwork. She'd spend a long time with Father learning how to tot up figures and she's very talented at that. Another useful thing.' She sighed and stood up. 'Lily, I wonder if you'd be so kind as to come with me to the church. Leave the mending. Talking about my parents makes me want to put some flowers on their grave. Eta brought me some early flowering primroses from the garden which I will take to the churchyard.'

23

Suitably wrapped up against the cold moonlit February evening, the two made their way slowly across the lane to the church. As they approached the grave, Mabel confided, 'Our parents were disappointed neither Eta nor I married. I can understand why no one wants me. I have neither looks nor health, but Eta is different. She's a strong woman, very capable, attractive and has a pleasant personality beneath her sternness.'

Lily thought about what Mabel said. If she were honest, she would admit that Mabel had summed herself up well and she admired her for it.

But Eta? She was a large woman, tall and stout, in direct contrast to her younger sister. If she had a pleasant personality she didn't show it willingly, at least not to anyone except Mabel. She was polite, but spoke her mind to customers most of the time, and if any stepped out of line, she told them off and they usually apologised. Her mahogany brown hair was her best feature, although Lily had spotted a few grey hairs, even

24

though Eta was probably only in her late thirties.

Mabel insisted on taking the last few steps on her own to the grave and Lily shivered under a tree waiting for her to let her know she was ready to return to the warmth of the house. Poor Mabel, she was a really kind person. It would be nice if she could find a husband, someone to devote himself to her with a different kind of love other than sisterly.

As the two women crossed the lane back to the house, a man appeared on a bicycle. He stopped and doffed his hat to them before carrying on to the beer house.

'What beautiful manners,' sighed Mabel. 'And so handsome a man.'

'He's very smartly dressed,' added Lily.

The two women giggled and Mabel slipped her arm through Lily's. 'I wonder if he's the husband I have been waiting for all these years.'

They entered the house and Lily took Mabel's coat and hung it up in the hall, leaving her to rest in the parlour.

'Lily, are you there?' Eta's voice was shrill and she sounded cross.

'I'm sorry, I've been to the churchyard with Miss Mabel.'

Eta's tone softened as she said, 'Well, now you'll have to come into the beer house as it's getting very busy and I need your help as I am on my own this evening.'

Lily smoothed down her apron and tucked stray strands of hair behind her ears. Normally, Lily didn't enjoy serving in the beer house, but she knew there was a chance to meet the stylish stranger on the bicycle.

He was standing by the counter draining a glass of beer. 'Good evening, another pint,' he said to Lily.

'Certainly, sir,' she replied, filling the glass carefully.

'We met in the lane, didn't we?'

'Yes, sir, you were on your bicycle.' She smiled at him. Mabel was right, he was handsome. A tall man with black hair and deep brown eyes. His rounded, clean-shaven face looked full of good humour. The pocket watch he produced to check the time looked expensive and he wore a gold ring. His clothes were well cut and Lily thought he must be well off. Overall he was an attractive, polite man, but with a tendency to put on weight, she thought.

'Do you do meals?' he asked.

Eta moved to Lily's side and told him they used to, but not any longer. 'I can offer you some bread and cold meat, if that's acceptable.'

'How kind of you to go to the trouble, especially when you are very busy here this evening.' He held out a hand to Eta. 'I am Cecil Potts, how do you do?'

Lily hid a smile as she saw Eta's cheeks turn pink when they shook hands. The evening in the beer house was quite entertaining for Lily now Cecil Potts had joined the gathering.

However, through the evening, Lily observed him giving unwanted attention to a couple of women waiting to be served at the counter. She didn't like it.

27

Near to the time Lily knew Eta wanted to close the beer house for the night, Cecil came to the counter, staggering a little, and asked for a refill of beer. Lily filled his glass and took the money he gave her. She calculated the change to give him, but he waved it aside. 'You keep it, I'm not short of cash.' Cecil leaned over Lily and his hand brushed against her chest. She backed away quickly and caught him half-smiling at her in a coarse way. Then he straightened up and glugged his drink.

'Tell me, who owns this place?'

'Miss Stratford,' Lily nodded towards Eta. 'I work for her and her sister.'

'Miss Stratford, you say? And her sister is a spinster also, is she?'

Putting his unexpected questions down to him having had too much to drink, Lily said that was right. 'They live in the house, do they? Just the two of them?'

Lily nodded, wondering how much she should tell Cecil. She decided there was nothing to be gained by letting him know she and Samuel lived there also. 'The Limes, it's called, the house.'

'Of course.' He finished his drink and lurched over to Eta. 'Goodnight, Miss Stratford, a pleasure to meet you. I shall come this way again and I look forward to seeing you.'

When he'd left, Eta said, 'You go into the house now, Lily, make sure Mabel is settled.' She put a hand on Lily's arm. 'Thank you for helping me this evening — and for going to the churchyard with Mabel.'

Lily was pleased to have finished her work at the beer house and hurried through to the house, where she saw Mabel was no longer in the parlour. She went upstairs and tapped on her bedroom door.

'Come in.'

'Miss Mabel, I'm sorry to be so late, but I have some gossip to tell you if you can stay awake long enough.'

Mabel yawned. 'I'm tired.' 'Cecil Potts was in the beer house.' Lily went on regardless.

'Who? I don't know him.' Mabel's eyes were already closing.

'The handsome stranger on the bicycle.'

Mabel shot up in bed. 'I am wide awake now! Tell me all you know.'

Lily recalled the evening at the beer house and described Cecil. Lily didn't want to disappoint Mabel by telling her about his flirting, so she just said, 'He's very good-looking and can be charming.'

'I wish I'd been there,' sighed Mabel. 'Do you think he'll call again?'

'Definitely. I heard him tell Miss Stratford he would come back.'

Eta entered the room, her face flushed. 'Are you all right?' Mabel asked.

'Of course. I have just come to wish you a good night, sister.'

'Lily has been telling me about a new customer, a Mr Potts.'

Eta frowned. 'Lily, you would do well to avoid gossiping. Please, go to bed. You have your usual early start tomorrow.'

Mabel made a face at her and smiled. As she left the room, Lily felt unsettled.

There was something about Mr Potts she didn't like. She particularly didn't like the way he had looked at, and touched, her in the beer house.

# 3

Lily continued to feel unsettled and there was a different atmosphere at The Limes which she could only put down to the fact that both the sisters had fallen in love with Cecil Potts. To her, his charm was superficial and she doubted his sincerity to her mistresses. It worried her that they were being enchanted by the man. He had become a frequent visitor at the house and showered both the sisters with compliments.

One evening Samuel was eating his meal with her in the kitchen after a day on his own in the fields painting. He was quiet and thoughtful, but Lily decided to talk to him about Cecil.

'Cecil called again today. With trinkets for Miss Stratford and Miss Mabel. They were both so excited and fussed over him. Mabel had made cakes especially for him. One of her interests as you know.'

32

'Are there any left?' Samuel asked.

Lily fetched a plateful and put them in front of him. 'There. When you have finished your stew, help yourself. She made more than enough. Even greedy Mr Potts couldn't eat them all.'

'Lily! I know you are joking. What do you make of him? Do you like him? Has he charmed you too? Are you attracted to him?' Samuel asked.

Lily was surprised at all the questions. 'I am not! Anyway, he's old enough to be my father. Miss Stratford and Mabel like him and have been flirting with him. Mabel thinks he has fallen for her sister and will ask her to marry him. She was cross and upset about it.'

'Will he make Eta a good husband? He is an insurance salesman and looks as though he does well financially. He has expensive tastes. Where does he live, do you know?'

'He has lodgings in town, but I've heard him say he'd like to live in a village like this. I really wish he hadn't turned up here. It's not pleasant now that Miss

33

Stratford and Mabel are fighting for his attention. If he does ask Miss Stratford to marry him there will be changes here at The Limes and not for the better.'

'Don't worry, Lily, whatever happens I'll be here to help.'

In spite of her misgivings, Lily felt a warmth spread through her and sat next to him.

Samuel moved nearer to her and put a hand on her shoulder. 'I wonder if you could care for someone like me?' he asked.

Surprised, Lily reached for his hand and he leaned towards her, his lips almost on hers. 'You said you didn't want company,' Lily said. 'You prefer solitude.'

'That was before I got to know you.'

'What if someone came and caught us close like this?'

Samuel dropped a kiss on her cheek.

'How's your arm?' Lily asked.

'It's much better, thank you. Would you like to see?' Just as he was about to take his shirt off, Mabel joined them in the kitchen.

'Lily, tidy up my hair, please. I think Cecil may be in the beer house drinking and I'd like a word with him, if Eta will let me and doesn't dominate the conversation.' Usually Mabel would be retiring to her room at this time, but her habits were changing. 'Come on now, Lily, use one of these ribbons. Cecil gave them to me and I'd like him to think I'm grateful for his generous gifts.'

She held out a bundle of ribbons and Lily took a green one and tied it in her hair. 'He gave Eta a beaded belt, you know. He's such a benevolent, bighearted and charming man. Don't you think so, Samuel?'

Samuel looked up from his meal. 'I don't know him as well as you, Mabel.'

'He is extremely handsome and confident, isn't he, Lily? And such a melodic voice. I do hope he will sing for us sometime soon. He works hard and is apparently well thought of by his customers. Such generosity too.'

Samuel smiled. 'A paragon! I must spend more time with him.'

Lily saw a glint in his clear blue eyes which suggested he was teasing, but Mabel was still dreaming about her ideal man.

'He smells of pine.' Mabel's face fell. 'He will ask Eta to marry him and I must not be jealous. I must be happy for her.'

'But you don't know that he will ask either of you to marry him,' Lily offered, knowing it wasn't her place to say so.

'I do. I would like to be Cecil's wife, I would like to be anybody's wife, but Eta deserves Cecil more than me. She is attractive, in good health and strong. They will make a fine couple, but I can enjoy his company as his friend and, later, his sister-in-law. I will go and join them.'

Lily took her basket of mending and sat by the range. 'Poor Mabel.'

'She is clearly in love. May I sit with you for a little while longer?' Samuel asked.

Lily nodded and he pulled another chair towards the warmth. 'I wonder why Cecil has suddenly appeared as if from nowhere,' she said.

'Perhaps he moved for his work.'

'Why is he wooing my mistresses?'

'They are both very fine women. Mabel may not be attractive or well, but she has many excellent qualities, especially her kindness. She and Eta helped me more than I could have imagined when my parents died. Without them I would be lost.'

'But there are many younger, more beautiful and amusing unmarried women locally. I don't understand his interest in them in particular.'

'It is a little confusing. Perhaps he is looking for a truly good woman. Or perhaps he has no intention of asking Eta to marry him. Perhaps it is a figment of their imagination!' He chuckled.

'I do hope so. There is something about him which makes me think he will only bring trouble to The Limes.'

'And what about you, Lily? How many times have you been asked to marry?'

Her cheeks felt hot. 'Never, not that it's any of your business.' After saying it she hoped she hadn't overstepped the line.

'Any man friends?' he continued.

'I used to go out with a boy from home, but when I came here we decided it would be impossible to continue. I expect he has already found someone else.'

'And you, Lily? Have you found someone else? Is there someone in the beer house perhaps?'

Her face felt hotter still. There was someone else, but she wasn't about to tell him. She longed to ask him about his love life, but felt it would be rude as she was just the maid after all.

'As for me, I haven't been looking for love. I have far too much to do, but I liked kissing you. Now I am going to my room.'

Lily was happy to sit in the kitchen working her way through the mending basket. It gave her time to relive her conversation with Samuel and think about his admission that he had no woman in his life. She longed to make him her own. She could dream, couldn't she?

# 4

Mabel was arranging greenery in the scullery and Lily could hear her singing. She had a sweet voice and sang in tune. It wasn't long before she appeared in the doorway holding a glass vase.

'Let me take that, it looks very heavy,' Lily offered.

'I feel strong today. Better than I've felt for a very long time, but let's sit for a bit and talk.' Mabel put the vase on the kitchen table and sat in one of the chairs. Lily had a lot to do, but didn't want to upset Mabel by not sitting with her.

'It's lovely that spring is here. I do like seeing the buds growing and hearing birds singing,' Mabel said.

'You seem very happy.'

'I am. Shall I tell you why?'

Lily could tell she was desperate to share whatever it was. 'If you'd like to.'

'It's Cecil. I think he's decided I'm the one for him. I can't believe I could have such good fortune.

He pays me the most wonderful compliments and many more than he pays Eta. I shouldn't really say this, it might be bad luck, but I have a feeling he's going to ask me to marry him.' She picked a dead leaf from her arrangement. Mabel appeared to have shed years.

'I'm very pleased for you,' Lily said.

'Of course someone won't be pleased.' Mabel nodded her head in the direction of the beer house where Eta was working. 'I know I shouldn't like it, but outdoing Eta for the first time in my life gives me a nice feeling. She will be devastated when he proposes to me.'

Lily was surprised at the turnaround of events as Mabel had been so convinced Cecil preferred Eta. Mabel was joyful and Lily desperately wanted to show her delight at the news, but she was fearful for her mistress's future if the marriage went ahead.

'I'm sure she will be happy for you when she sees your joy.'

'I never thought a man, and especially

one as wonderful as Cecil, would ever pay me any attention. I keep having to pinch myself.'

Lily wondered why Cecil Potts had been interested in either Miss Stratford, but if he was to marry one of them surely he would have chosen the older sister.

Mabel surprised Lily by saying she was going to the beer house. Then, of course, she realised it was to see Cecil. 'Come through with me, Lily. I won't stay long as I know Eta will want me to return to the house.'

Lily felt awkward standing doing nothing in the beer house while Eta filled a shelf and Mabel talked to her sister. Cecil walked into the beer house and joined them. 'Ladies,' he said, 'how beautiful you both look.'

Eta blushed, and Mabel smiled and looked at the floor. Briefly, Lily was aware of Cecil's eyes on her, but when she met his stare, he looked away. 'I'd like these goods, hurry and serve me.'

Both sisters rushed to him, but Mabel got there first. 'I'll serve you, Cecil,' said

41

Mabel, taking the bread and some eggs he had chosen.

He smiled. Mabel told him how much he owed and he took some coins from his pocket. 'Here you are.'

'Thank you. And it is a pleasure doing business with you. It's always a delight to see you. Would you like to come to the house for a cup of tea?'

Eta frowned at her, but said nothing.

'Nothing would delight me more. Take my arm and I will help you.'

Lily could tell from the look on Mabel's face that she was thrilled, but she couldn't help thinking Cecil was enjoying Mabel's flattering manner towards him. 'Shall I go back into the house as well, Miss Mabel? I've still a lot of work to do.'

'Yes, please, Lily.'

As soon as they got into The Limes, Mabel took Cecil into the parlour and asked Lily to make them some tea.

'Something to eat, too, Mabel, anything other than that cake I had,' Cecil said.

If Lily had a sharp object she'd have poked it in his eye. That was very rude and poor Mabel looked near tears. When she came back with the tea, but nothing to eat, she was relieved to see the two were getting on better. Cecil was saying how clever Mabel must be to play the piano and he wished he could. But Lily had witnessed the nasty sides of Cecil and she wondered if there were any more hidden below his usually charming surface.

While Lily was cleaning the downstairs of the house, she overheard Eta, who must have closed the shop to spend time with Cecil, asking him about his work.

'You don't need to concern yourself with things like that, dear lady. I earn a decent wage and am well-thought of at my work place.'

'Do stop questioning the man, Eta,' Lily heard Mabel tell her sister. 'He doesn't want to think about work when he's here relaxing with me — that is, us.'

'I am enjoying being here,' said Cecil,

'but it is time for me to leave you both and go about my business.'

Lily ducked into the dining room so she wouldn't be found in the hallway and thought to be eavesdropping, which she was.

Shortly after Cecil had left, Eta went back to the beer house and shop, telling Lily she would need her in the beer house during the evening, and Mabel went up to her bedroom for a rest.

Everything at The Limes went on as usual until quite late at night when there was a sharp rap at the door. Eta, who had been on the point of retiring to bed, told Mabel and Lily she'd answer it. It was Cecil and he came into the parlour seeming as if he'd had too much to drink. Quite a bit too much, in Lily's opinion. She decided to stay with the sisters in case there was trouble and she wished Samuel was with them. He was probably in his room and Lily wondered about fetching him.

'I've got to be on my way,' slurred Cecil, staggering into the hall.

44

'Lily, get some tea for Mr Potts.' As Lily left the room, she heard Eta saying to Mabel they must try to sober him up as best they could. 'He drinks far too much, it's not a good quality in anyone.'

'Leave him alone, Eta,' said Mabel, 'He works very hard and deserves to relax. You don't mind taking his money in the beer house,' she said, quite un-Mabel-like. She went into the hall and said, 'Come now, dear Cecil, we aren't letting you go home until you've had some tea.' He succumbed and allowed himself to be led back into the parlour.

When Lily returned with the tea, Cecil and Mabel were sitting close together and Mabel was gazing at him lovingly. His eyes were closed and he looked as though he was about to fall asleep. It suddenly struck Lily that Cecil may have turned his attention from the more dominant sister to the more submissive one because he would be able to control her.

By April, there was great excitement at The Limes as Mabel was to be married to Cecil. Although she was delighted to be included with the sisters in choosing a suitable dress for Mabel to wear for the most important day of her life, Lily was unsure whether happiness would follow the day. She couldn't imagine anything worse than being with someone like Cecil for a lifetime. Her thoughts drifted to Samuel, who hadn't been very enthusiastic about the marriage news, but had said he hoped Mabel would be happy. It was difficult to know what to say to Eta as she was clearly disappointed at not being the bride. Samuel had said he was sure Mabel would turn to her older, wiser sister for help and advice as she always had done, and Eta had calmed down at his considerate words.

The three women were in Lily's room examining the contents of one of the wardrobes. 'Mother's clothes,' explained Mabel. 'Oh, I remember that one, and that one.' She let her hand float along the material, stopping now and then to pull at a garment, examine it and let it fall back into line. 'I'm sure we'll find something here.'

'I'm surprised Cecil didn't offer to pay for a new dress,' sniffed Eta. 'He's keen to let people know he's not short of money.'

'I expect he thought I'd be happier in one of Mother's dresses, and I do like the idea as she won't be with me on my wedding day. This way, she'll feel close,' said Mabel, making excuses as usual for Cecil. 'Don't forget he's paying for the food.'

Lily looked at Eta and they frowned. From what Lily had heard, the budget Cecil had given them wouldn't feed a church mouse.

'You're right, Mabel, but don't you forget you're making your own wedding cake and paying for the ingredients.'

'That's because Cecil says he cannot imagine a more delicious cake than one of my making. I shall enjoy doing it and be proud to see it on display. It's my gift to Cecil.'

Lily thought back to the time he'd asked not to have more of her cake. What was going on? He was getting more hateful as each layer of him unfolded.

Mabel suddenly shrieked. 'This is the one. The colour is perfect and I remember Mother wearing it and it still smells of her.' She gathered the dress to her face and breathed in deeply. 'Violets, they always remind me of Mother.'

Mabel held the dusky pink dress up to herself and swayed in front of the mirror letting the material float backwards and forwards. Lily thought it too fussy with its frills, flounces, and lace ruffles over the skirt and at the high neck and wrists.

'Stand still, Mabel,' Eta said. 'How can we see anything with you waltzing around?'

Mabel stood still and Eta held it closer to her.

'It's going to need altering. Lily, you can see to that, can't you? Fetch your pins and Mabel will put the dress on for you to fit it.'

Lily rushed off to fetch the pins. She felt sure her hands would shake as altering the dress was a big responsibility.

Suppose she made a mistake and ruined it? As she crossed the landing, Samuel bounded up the stairs.

'Lily, what's the matter? You look unhappy.'

'They want me to alter one of Mabel's mother's dresses so that it can be her wedding dress. I'm worried I'll make a mistake and she will look like one of the sacks of potatoes in the shop.'

Samuel grinned. 'I have seen your skill at needlework. You have a talent. If anyone can make Mabel look like a princess on her wedding day, it's you. Now, off you go, they will be waiting for you.'

As Lily tried to push past him, Samuel moved the same way and blocked her. He was so near, she could smell his scent — nothing fancy like Cecil wore, just clean skin and freshly washed hair. Try as she might, she couldn't get past him. Didn't want to, was probably nearer the mark. He pulled her towards him. 'You're adorable, Lily. I get more fond of you every time I see you. I even find you're a distraction when I'm trying to paint. What's to be done about it?'

Not knowing what was happening, Lily lifted her lips to his mouth briefly. Then she fled downstairs for the pins.

When she went back into the room, the two sisters were once again looking through the wardrobe. 'We're looking for a suitable dress for my maid of honour,' Mabel explained.

Eta pulled out a pale blue dress. 'This is a beautiful one.' Lily had to agree and once Eta had put it on there was no comparison with her younger sister. She looked majestic and striking. The dress was low cut and fitted tightly below her bust. The over layer of material was delicate chiffon and Lily thought the way it hung over the skirt must be like waves in the sea. The sleeves came to below her elbow and showed her well-shaped forearms. It fitted perfectly. 'What do you think, Mabel?' she asked.

'I think it's lovely, but you won't outdo the bride, I'm afraid, sister dear. Won't Cecil be delighted when I walk down the aisle and he turns and sees me?'

Eta nodded, removed the dress and sat on the bed. 'Come along now, Lily, do what you can.'

Still trembling from her kiss with Samuel, Lily pinned the dress while the two women talked.

'Think how happy Mother would be were she still alive. She always hoped we would marry. I expect someone might turn up for you one day, Eta, but you'll never have good fortune such as mine. Any woman would be pleased to marry my Cecil.'

Lily took a pin from her mouth and made another tuck. The thought of marrying Cecil turned her stomach. Everything about him sickened her.

'We must find some jewellery to go with your dress. Mother's jewellery box is in my room,' Eta said. 'I'll fetch it and we'll find something beautiful for you to wear.'

Lily continued with her task until Eta returned and tipped the jewellery out on the bed.

'Stop for a moment, Lily.' Mabel

walked over to the bed. 'This is perfect.' She held up a silver heart-shaped locket on a chain. 'I remember Mother wearing it. It has pictures of Mother and Father inside. Isn't it exquisite, Lily?'

Lily thought it was wonderful and nodded.

Eta scooped the rest of the jewellery back into the box. 'Samuel will feel proud walking you down the aisle,' she said. 'I am delighted he accepted your invitation.' Eta took Mabel's hand and said, 'I am very pleased to see you as happy as you are, dear sister. Mother and Father would be too. You deserve happiness because you give it.' Then she kissed Mabel's cheek.

As she carried on pinning the dress, Lily imagined Samuel in his Sunday best with Mabel's arm in his. He would give her a reassuring smile and lead Mabel to marry the man Lily was sure would ruin her life.

# 5

Lily felt the overcast April day was symbolic of the time ahead. She was busy preparing the wedding breakfast, as she had been for the past few days. Samuel came into the kitchen.

'I'm trying to keep out of the way,' he explained. 'Eta and Mabel are behaving like excited kittens. They both look pretty, though.'

'You look very handsome yourself, Samuel,' said Lily, looking at his freshly washed hair and scrubbed face. He was wearing a suit. She was used to him in his everyday clothes, but dressed up he was particularly eye-catching. It was a change, but she still liked the old Samuel. 'May I ask you something?'

He sat at the kitchen table. 'Of course.'

'Why were you asked to give Mabel away?'

'As you know, my parents are dead. My family and the Stratfords were great friends, that's how I came to lodge here. They asked me. So I suppose I'm the nearest Mabel has to a male relative.'

As Lily looked at Samuel's elegant appearance, she thought Cecil wouldn't be able to compete with him. She raced to the garden and came back with a purple pansy which she put in Samuel's buttonhole. Being so close made her feel dizzy and she had to resist the temptation to hold onto his shoulders. 'I hope you don't mind,' she said.

Samuel looked down at his buttonhole. 'Very pretty, thank you. It's perfect. Just like you.' He cupped her cheeks in his hands and kissed her. Lily felt lightheaded and didn't want to get through the day without him near her.

Lily sighed. 'I wish I could be at the church to see everything.'

'Can't you come across, just for a few minutes?'

'I dare not, I've been told everything must be ready when you all come back. There's so much to do. I shouldn't be here gossiping with you.'

'I enjoy talking to you, Lily. Shall we pretend there isn't a wedding today and run off somewhere with a picnic?'

Lily's heart leapt. It would be her dream and she spent a few moments thinking about it. Then she laughed. 'What a good idea. I'll leave you to explain to Eta, shall I?'

Samuel laughed with her then walked to the door. 'I'd better go. See you later.'

Left alone once more, Lily felt disappointed Mabel hadn't suggested she went to the church for the ceremony. Although they couldn't be counted as friends, Lily thought the two of them had become quite close.

When Lily heard the sisters come down the stairs, she went into the hallway. 'Miss Mabel, how pretty you look.' It was amazing to see Mabel dressed in her pink wedding dress. It fitted perfectly thanks to Lily's needlework skills. She had a veil over her face, and the bouquet of lilies of the valley from the garden was eye-catching. Mabel had made the bouquet herself and wound the stems in a length of white ribbon which Cecil had given her.

'Thank you, Lily. My stomach is very jittery.'

'That's usual, so I'm told,' said Eta. 'But Lily is right, you do look very pretty. This marriage is all very quick, Mabel, but I do hope you will be happy.'

'I will be, Eta. Thank you.'

Samuel came into the hallway. 'It's time to walk over to the church,' he said. 'Such a shame the sun's not shining.'

While the wedding ceremony was taking place, Lily checked the food, glad to have the house to herself in which to worry over her cooking. If her writing was better, she would have made a list of all the things she'd made, but she had to trust her memory and hope she didn't forget anything. She had cooked a joint of beef, some tongue, a large beef and oyster suet pudding and some chicken pies. Vegetables had been laid ready for boiling when the guests arrived at the house. There was also the cake which Mabel had made, and Lily had put together a walnut pudding and a large dish of trifle. She couldn't help thinking there wouldn't have been nearly such a spread if Eta hadn't added to Cecil's meagre contribution for the food.

Lily tried to imagine the bridal pair at the church; Mabel and Eta were suitably clothed, each in one of their mother's dresses, and Samuel was smart and handsome in his suit, but she wondered what Cecil would wear. And she had no idea who his best man would be. Cecil was bringing a life's dream to Mabel and he didn't appear to have a hidden reason, so Lily must learn to accept him and serve him as she did Eta and Mabel.

The church bells pealed for the second time that morning and Lily knew the couple were now man and wife. She looked out of the window, hoping for a little ray of sunshine, but there was none. Clouds looked down on the village and the atmosphere was gloomy. The wedding party would soon be at the house and Lily was ready.

Mabel and Cecil, who was wearing

a dark grey jacket and trousers, with a light-coloured waistcoat, came in first. A man, dressed like Cecil, followed them in. She assumed he was the best man. The men both looked smart. Following behind were Eta, her arm in Samuel's, and some of the villagers and people from outlying farms whom Lily recognised from the beer house and shop. It seemed the vicar, Harold Mason, had accepted an invitation to the wedding breakfast as well. Everyone was smiling and laughing and Mabel, especially, looked very happy, her face lighting up with a smile which spread across her mouth and up to her eyes.

As Lily made her way between the kitchen and the dining room, she thought that there was no one, apart from the best man, whom she'd found out was only an acquaintance from the beer house, from Cecil's side.

'Lily, this is a magnificent spread.' Samuel was standing near the door and took a laden plate from Lily to lay on the table with the other dishes.

'I hope it tastes good. And I hope there's enough.' Lily began to worry again before telling herself she had done the best with what she had been given. She went back to the kitchen and realised Samuel was following her. They sat down and Lily let out a sigh. After a couple of minutes, she said, 'Samuel, don't you think it's strange that Cecil has invited no one?'

'I do. I was wondering that when he was standing with the virtual stranger near the altar.' A mischievous look came into Samuel's eyes. 'Shall I ask him?'

'About his family?' Lily giggled. 'If you dare.'

They carried the rest of the food into the dining room and Lily fussed over a dish of fruit while Samuel approached Cecil.

'Congratulations, Cecil,' he said. 'This is a fine gathering, isn't it? But you don't seem to have invited many people. Couldn't your family get here?'

'Mind your own business. It's nothing to do with you.' Cecil was abrupt to the point of rudeness and brushed Samuel aside before helping himself to a glass of beer.

After all the guests had left, Lily cleared up and was finally able to sit down and kick off her shoes. She didn't intend doing any more work that evening, not even mending. Samuel came in saying Eta had asked for some warm milk as her stomach was troubling her. Lily was about to stand to fetch it, but Samuel said, 'No, no, Lily, you have worked quite hard enough today. You did a good job and deserve a rest. I will get Eta's drink and once I have taken it to her in the parlour I will return and make you something. I think the happy couple will be retiring soon and Eta won't be far behind them. There should be no more demands made on you.'

Lily watched him as he moved around the kitchen. Just as he was about to leave, Cecil walked in. The atmosphere changed.

'You should finish clearing up,' he told her.

'I have.'

'I'll have none of your cheek. You'd do well to remember who is master of this house now. I want the furniture all moved back to its correct position.'

'Miss Stratford said it could be left until tomorrow when I could have some help.'

'You'll do as you're told. Get a move on.' He turned and left the room.

Lily thought Samuel looked annoyed. His fists were clenched and a frown crossed his face. She dragged herself out of the chair, forced her shoes back on and made her way to the dining room. As she started to move a table Samuel joined her and silently helped. When they had finished in the dining room they went towards the parlour. In the hallway Samuel put his hand on her arm to stop her. They listened at the bottom of the stairs as Cecil shouted at Mabel upstairs.

'We should have the biggest room,' he bellowed.

They strained their ears to hear Mabel's reply. 'I like this room. It's always been mine.'

'You're married now, not some silly young girl.'

'The biggest room is Lily's and I'm not prepared to move her.'

'Not prepared to move your maid! You clearly have no idea how to be the mistress of this house. You'll have to buck up.'

Lily couldn't bear to listen any longer. She was sorry for Mabel and wondered how she had been taken in by the man. Looking down she realised Samuel's hand was still on her arm. They smiled at each other and he followed her into the parlour.

In her room at last, it took Lily a long time to drop off to sleep as she was thinking about her time spent with Samuel that day as well as the rest of the celebration. Her mother would love to hear about it all. It was a pity she lived so far away and Lily, being unable to write well enough, couldn't communicate by letter. How she wished she'd been able to stay on at school to learn more than just the very basics of reading and writing instead of having to leave to help with the younger children at home.

Eventually she fell asleep.

The morning brought its usual routine of cleaning and breakfast preparation. When Lily went into the dining room with cutlery and napkins, she was surprised to see Mabel sitting at the table. 'Miss Mabel, I didn't hear you come down, shall I bring your breakfast now?'

'I'll wait, thank you, Lily. And please don't forget I'm Mrs Mabel Potts now.'

Lily had forgotten and wondered if she'd ever get used to saying Mrs Potts or Mrs Mabel. Eta and Samuel took their places at the table.

Back in the kitchen, Lily piled dishes with hot food and made a pot of tea which she took through to the dining room. The usual chatter of breakfast was absent, and Cecil was sitting at the head of the table. Mabel seemed even more timid, and shrunk into herself.

'Bring the food, girl, I'm hungry,' Cecil said, tucking a napkin at his neck.

'Her name is Lily,' said Eta, glaring at

her brother-in-law.

'I'll call her what I like, Henrietta — you too.'

Lily hurried to get the food on the sideboard and inadvertently dropped a piece of ham on the floor. Bending to pick it up, she was aware of Samuel by her side. He gave a small smile and winked at her.

'Don't waste food, girl,' said Cecil, watching her closely.

'Sorry, Mr Potts.' Lily fled, glad to be out of the nasty atmosphere. She hoped it wouldn't be like this every day now Cecil Potts had come to live with them.

From the kitchen window, Lily was glad to see him getting on his bicycle and pedalling away from the house. She let out a sigh of relief and went to collect the dirty breakfast dishes.

'Sorry, Miss . . . Mrs Potts, I didn't realise you were still in here. Shall I come back later?'

'No, Lily, I've finished, thank you, although I only had some tea and a small piece of bread.'

'Are you unwell this morning?'

'Just a bit tired. It was a busy day yesterday.' Mabel stood up. 'Lily, I wonder if you could help me tidy some drawers in the bedroom to make room for Cecil's things. Finish what you have to do in the kitchen first, of course. I'll go up and wait for you.'

Lily found Mabel sitting on the edge of the bed looking pale. 'You just sit there and tell me what you'd like me to do.'

To Lily's horror Mabel burst into tears and buried her head in her hands.

'Miss Mabel, please don't cry. Shall I come back later?'

'No, please stay, Lily.' She sniffed and wiped her nose and eyes with a handkerchief. 'I need to ask you something, something quite delicate.'

'Of course, I don't mind what you ask. I will do my best to help.'

'Well, last night, in bed with Cecil, well, I'm not sure how to phrase this, but he was quite rough with me and I wondered if that was normal.'

Lily was shocked. 'I have no experience, but it's an act of love and so I

65

always imagined it would be tender and gentle.'

Mabel nodded. 'Thank you, Lily. Look.' She rolled up her sleeves to reveal livid bruises on her upper arms. 'Please don't tell Eta.'

The sight of Mabel's distress and the bruises upset Lily and she wanted to tell someone about it, but she didn't want to break a confidence.

After she'd sorted out some drawer space for Cecil's belongings, Lily carried on as usual, unable to rid her mind of him being so cruel and unloving towards Mabel, his new bride. She was sure Samuel would never behave that way. He was always kind and considerate of other people's feelings. Thinking of him, she wondered where he was as she hadn't seen him since breakfast.

Samuel wasn't around at the evening meal. He was probably off in the woods painting again. Exhausted, mentally and physically, Lily sat in the kitchen and began her solitary meal.

'Hello, may I join you, please?'

'Samuel, I wondered where you were. You must be hungry. Let me get you a plateful of food.'

'I can get it, you carry on with your meal.' He piled his plate with chicken and home-grown vegetables. 'Your cooking is always delicious, Lily,' he said, sitting opposite her.

'Thank you.'

'I didn't come home until I knew the meal in the dining room would be finished. I just can't stand being in the same room as that awful man. I stayed out of the way, hiding.' He laughed. 'Isn't that a silly thing to do?'

'No, it was very sensible of you.'

'I'm glad you're here. I enjoy being with you, Lily. I think I'll make a habit of coming in late so I can have more meals with you.'

'I'd like that.' Lily put the empty plates in the sink. When she turned, Samuel was behind her. His face came close to hers and their lips met.

# 6

Lily sang as she cleaned Mabel and Cecil's room. Cecil had a habit of leaving his things untidily and she always found work to do in their room. Samuel had done as he'd said and avoided meals with the others.

He spent his evenings with her. She had never been in love before, but her feelings for Samuel were growing.

As she tidied the newly married couple's things away, thoughts of mean, bullying Cecil replaced those of kind, gentle, thoughtful Samuel.

Almost as though she had conjured him up by thinking about him, Cecil suddenly entered the room.

'Pretty singing, girl,' he said, moving closer to her.

'Thank you, Mr Potts.' She had vowed to be polite to him for Mabel's sake, but inside she seethed. His treatment of Mabel appalled her.

He moved to the bed and sat on it. 'Come now, sit here next to me,' he said, patting the quilt beside him.

'I have work to do, Mr Potts, I don't have time to sit and I wouldn't sit on a bed next to you. It would be wrong.'

'Wrong, eh?' he replied. 'But you'd like to get close, wouldn't you? Don't you think the way you have looked at me is wrong? You with your big brown cow eyes, gazing at me whenever you think no one else is looking. I have seen you! For me to even talk to you is beneath me. You should take it as a great kindness that I am showing an interest in you. We can have a nice time together, Lily dear. We can be together regularly. I can come to your room at night.'

Lily vowed she would put a chair under her bedroom door handle when she was in her room. She glanced at the door. Could she get there without him grabbing her?

'I'm waiting for you, girl.' He tugged at his necktie and pulled it off, then he started to roll up his shirt sleeves. 'Are

69

you jealous of my other women? I suppose that's natural, but I shall allow you to share my attentions.'

Lily was angry. 'Other women? You have a wife, you should be faithful to her. She is a wonderful woman and deserves a happy life. You are a very lucky man.' Lily knew it wasn't her place to speak to him like that. However, she was feeling desperate and needed to get out of the room and away from him.

'Not going to give in easily, eh? I like spirit. Want me to fight for your favours, do you?' He lunged forward and grabbed her wrist. As she tried to struggle free, he held her tightly and pushed his face against hers. 'There now. Ready to give in?'

His breath smelt rancid and she gagged. What could she do? His mouth came nearer to hers. She decided that, even if she lost her job, she would bite him.

'Ceciiil!' Suddenly, Eta was calling from the bottom of the stairs.

Cecil let go, pushing Lily away from him. 'My dear sister-in-law. She too would have married me had I asked. You'd do well to remember I'm a well-respected man. Keep quiet and we'll get together some other time.'

Lily was upset, yet furious. 'Stay away from me or else! Do you hear me?'

'I hear you, dear girl. Just remember that I'm the master and you're the maid.' Cecil laughed and left the room.

During the next week, Lily tried to keep as far away from Cecil as possible. It wasn't easy. She was just congratulating herself on how well she was doing when he walked into the kitchen.

'Aha, there you are. Alone at last. Shall we start where we left off? Put down that pan and come with me.'

'I will not.' She felt like bashing him over the head with the pan. That would stop him!

He seized her arm, removed the pan from her hand and held her tightly. 'Now, be a good girl. Come with me.'

'What on earth!' Eta suddenly stood in the doorway. 'What do you think you're doing, Cecil? Let Lily go.'

'I thought she looked pale and some fresh air would do her good. I was simply taking her into the garden.'

Once released, Lily almost fell into a chair. She wanted to scrub her arm clean where Cecil had held her.

Eta moved towards Lily and put a hand on her shoulder. 'I don't believe you. I saw the look on Lily's face and the way you were holding her. It is appalling! And you married such a short time. My poor sister! You had better behave properly or you'll be sorry.'

Cecil laughed. 'And what can you do? Nothing. I shall join my charming wife in the parlour. I expect she's being weak and sickly there, the poor thing.'

When he'd left the kitchen, Eta said, 'Lily, I will keep you safe. Let me make you a soothing drink.'

In spite of Miss Stratford's reassurance and kindness, Lily felt as though she couldn't breathe. 'I must get some air.' She rushed out into the garden and threw herself on the grass under one of the lime trees. When the sound of someone approaching disturbed the silence, the thought of Cecil coming to get her made her cry and shake.

'Lily! I found you.' It was Samuel. He sat beside her and wiped her tears away with his fingers. 'What's wrong?'

'Oh, it's nothing. I did a few silly things today and I feel foolish. I'll be fine.' She wanted to tell Samuel the truth, but the thought of him becoming violent towards Cecil stopped her.

'You mustn't feel foolish, Lily. We all do silly things.' Samuel plucked at the grass. 'I can't seem to paint very well lately, I think you're distracting me.'

'Me?' Lily tried to smile, but her lips couldn't stop quivering.

He put an arm around her shoulders. 'I don't like to see you upset.'

She nodded. 'I will tell you as I'm worried about Mabel. Oh dear, I shall never get used to thinking of her as anything else. To call her Mrs Potts, the wife of that monster, makes me feel ill.'

As she started to tremble again, Samuel's arms came around her and she nestled into the comfort of his chest. 'It's a pity he came to this house. And he's lucky I haven't killed him yet.'

Despite everything, Lily giggled and looked up at him. 'Run him through with your paintbrush, would you?'

Samuel let out a bellow of laughter. 'Oh, Lily, I wish I could help you.'

Without hesitating, Lily poured out the details which Mabel had told her following her wedding night with Cecil.

For a long while, Samuel was silent. Eventually, he said, 'I've seen him in the beer house flattering and touching women customers. Most of them appear not to like it, but they say nothing. I thought it would stop after he was married. As you know, I avoid him as much as possible, but I have just visited the shop to see if Eta needed some sacks lifting, and Cecil was in a distasteful conversation with a woman; he had his back to me and had no idea I was there.'

'Didn't Eta say anything to him?'

'She didn't notice. There were lots of customers and she said she wasn't going to ask you to go and help. Some of the women enjoy his attentions, of course,' added Samuel.

'But he's married.' Lily couldn't understand the way some people lived. She wasn't used to this sort of thing. Her parents and brothers were responsible, considerate people who behaved well, as she herself tried to do. If she told Samuel about Cecil wanting to bed her, would he think she had encouraged him?

'Yes, and I wish I could do away with him.' Samuel frowned and his knuckles grew white as he clasped his fingers into a fist.

'I really should get back to work,' she said, standing up.

Samuel scrambled off the grass and put his hands to Lily's face. 'You still look very unhappy.'

'I'll be all right. Thank you, Samuel, you've helped me.' Lily didn't like keeping things from Samuel, but she didn't want to be responsible for what might happen if she told him what Cecil had tried to do to her.

# 7

Lily continued with her duties and Eta was her protector from Cecil. Samuel still avoided mealtimes in the dining room as far as he could, but he explained to Lily that he'd decided he should be there sometimes if only to defend the Stratford sisters, if need be, from Cecil. The following months passed, if not completely harmoniously, a bit better than Lily had anticipated.

'It will be Christmas soon,' said Eta. 'We must have a tree and decorate it and I'm sure Mabel will be able to make some floral arrangements'

Lily wondered what Cecil would make of the extra expense of Christmas, but luckily, he was away from the house often.

'I'll try to make something,' said Mabel, 'but I'm not sure if I should go out in the cold and icy weather. What if I slip?'

'I'll go and get what you'd like, Mrs Potts,' offered Lily. 'Yes, let Lily go,' said Eta. 'She likes being in the garden, even in December.'

Lily sat with Mabel in the parlour and they talked about what was available in their garden. There was holly and ivy and they decided to ask Samuel if he could gather some mistletoe from the top of the lime trees as well as anything suitable from the woods when he ventured out in the cold to paint.

'May I have some tea, Lily?' Mabel sank back in her chair and closed her eyes.

'Yes, Mrs Potts. Do you feel ill?'

'I'm very tired, but I hear that's what happens when one is expecting a baby.'

Lily went to the kitchen and made a potful of tea which she brought to Mabel. She added a piece of cake which she'd made the previous day. Mabel had sat with her in the kitchen while she'd mixed it, saying it was the nearest she got to baking these days. When Lily returned to the parlour with the refreshments for

Mabel, she found Eta there. 'Miss Stratford, I'll fetch another cup and slice of cake. I didn't expect you.'

'I came to see how Mabel was.' She rubbed her sister's back gently and smiled at her.

'I'm fine. I must be all right to help you, Eta. I'm not doing enough.'

'Don't you dare say that. You do a marvellous job here in the house and in the shop.'

'Cecil doesn't seem to think so. He keeps finding fault with me, saying that I'm not earning my keep.'

'He doesn't keep you, Mabel, we have always looked after each other, you and I, and we will continue to do so. You must make sure that you rest enough. It will be so lovely to have a baby in the house.'

Mabel continued to look miserable. A few minutes later, Cecil burst into the room.

'There are customers in the shop, Eta, and Bertha is useless and can't serve them all. Do you think we have enough money that you can just ignore them?

We'll soon have another mouth to feed.'

Eta went back to the shop and Cecil said he'd have some tea and cake. When Lily came back from the kitchen, he was saying to Mabel, 'We don't need any special things for Christmas. Lily can make the food just as she did for our wedding breakfast, although on a much smaller and cheaper scale, of course. I expect the shop and beer house will be open on Christmas Day.'

'Who would want to go out of their homes and drink alcohol on Christmas Day?'

Cecil slurped his tea and munched his cake. 'Don't keep questioning me,' he said, his mouth still full. 'You will attend church, work and have a meal. I don't expect any fancy decorations or fripperies.'

'We always play games. It is a wonderful day for us.'

'Wonderful? You think of playing games. A married woman expecting a child. There will be no games in your master's house.'

Lily was pleased that in the days before Christmas, Cecil was out a lot. She didn't care where he was as long as he wasn't making the sisters miserable. When he was in the house he didn't help in any way, but did drink in the beer house. Each time Eta and Mabel were sure he was out their mood appeared to rise and they laughed together. However, with Mabel unwell and not able to do a lot, Lily was worn out with work as she spent a lot of time with Mabel each day and had to get the household jobs completed as well.

'How are you this morning?' she asked, when she went into Mabel and Cecil's bedroom.

'I feel unwell, but Cecil has gone out and I may get up later.' She rested her hand on the mound of her stomach. 'I am looking forward to meeting our baby. It's exciting to think we will have a new member of the family.'

'And Mr Potts?'

'Oh, Lily, you know he just sees the child as a further expense and nuisance.

I often lie here and question why he married me. But,' she sat up, 'I have told him intimacy will harm the baby and he believes me. He isn't happy about it, but he leaves me alone which is a huge relief.'

'That was a clever idea. I am pleased for you. I too am excited about the baby and, as you know, Miss Stratford is delighted.'

'She would have liked a child, but she will be a wonderful aunt and will treat it as if it were her own. The baby will be loved by us, even if not by his father.'

'Do you think it will be a boy?' Lily asked.

'I'm not sure, but I think a boy might just bring Cecil round to showing an interest.'

'How different our lives will be with a baby in the house.'

'How different our lives have been since I married Cecil. There is very little joy here. I am dreading Christmas more than looking forward to it. Cecil will make the atmosphere gloomy. And all of us in it.'

'Then we mustn't allow it, Mrs Potts. We must make sure we have an enjoyable and lively time.'

Despite Lily's promise, Christmas Day was more depressing than any of them imagined. It was bitterly cold and Eta tried to keep the fires supplied with logs from the outhouse which Samuel chopped into smaller pieces. All Cecil did was sit around the house, being rude to them. Mabel was unable to persuade him to do anything. Lily and Samuel huddled in the kitchen trying to ignore the icy weather and equally icy atmosphere. Everyone was pleased when Christmas was over.

'A new year to look forward to, Lily,' said Samuel.

'I hope it will be better than this one.'

'You look very unhappy.' He cupped her chin in his hand. 'What is it?'

Tears pricked Lily's eyes. 'I miss my mum,' she said. 'It's ages since I've seen her or had any news from the family. They'll forget what I look like,' she sniffed.

'Then I shall paint your picture! I shall

bring my painting things down into the kitchen and paint a picture of a beautiful young lady.'

Lily didn't think she was at all beautiful, but it cheered her to hear Samuel's words. He was the kindest, most thoughtful man she'd ever met and she was pleased she'd be spending even more time with him.

It was a cold February day when Lily heard Mabel calling from her room. She rushed up the stairs almost colliding with Eta at the bedroom door.

'What is it, Mabel? Is the baby coming?' Eta asked.

All Mabel could do was groan as a pain ripped through her. Sweat beaded her brow and she clutched at the bedclothes.

Eta immediately took charge.

'Lily, run for the midwife, then come back upstairs as we'll need your help fetching things. Don't worry about a meal, the men will have to fend for themselves.'

It wasn't long before the midwife

handed Mabel her baby swaddled tightly in a sheet. 'A beautiful girl,' she said.

Eta looked down at her sister and the baby with tears in her eyes. 'Isn't she beautiful, Mabel?'

Just as she said the words, Mabel thrust the baby at her sister as she howled with pain.

'There's another on the way,' the midwife said.

'Another?' Eta moved to a chair and sat down clutching the precious bundle.

'What will Cecil say?' Mabel sobbed between contractions.

'Twins,' was all Lily could murmur.

Very soon the second baby, a boy, arrived. 'Two healthy babies, both look good weights and with lusty lungs. The father will be a very happy man. Double the trouble, double the joy.'

When the midwife had left Mabel closed her eyes. 'I'm exhausted.'

'You must be. What will you call them? Or will Cecil name them?' Eta asked.

'I will name them. They are Sylvan

and Archie.'

Eta who was now cradling both babies looked besotted. 'Archie and Sylvan. Hello. Welcome to the world. I hope it will be kind to you.'

As Lily tidied up she felt sadness for Eta who would probably never have children of her own. She would have been a good mother. Lily fell to wondering if she would ever want children. She might, but for now she would be contented with her life. If only Cecil wasn't around. She missed her family, but she was able to help them by sending home money. Samuel entered her thoughts. She would find him and tell him about the babies. If she were ever to have children Samuel would be the man she'd want them with. That's a nice prospect, she thought.

The arrival of not only one, but two babies at The Limes was a mixed blessing. Mabel struggled to look after them. 'I'm a terrible mother,' she moaned one day to Lily who had come to help her feed the babies. Usually, Lily held one of the twins and Mabel fed the other, thus keeping them both happy. Mabel's milk was slow to come and it tired her when she was feeding. 'I shall have to give them some cow's milk,' she declared.

'Is that all right?' asked Lily, who had no idea what to advise.

Eta stood by and wrung her hands when she witnessed her sister's dilemma. 'This is something I can't help you with,' she said. 'I'm sure it will get easier as you get used to feeding.'

'It's not just feeding, is it?' wailed Mabel. 'It's everything else as well. I cannot manage. Please don't let Cecil know, he won't like it if I can't take care of the babies and do what I used to do.'

Eta and Lily exchanged a look over Sylvan's head and Lily was sure she knew Eta was thinking the same thing she was: Cecil would take it out on his wife if she failed in her duties.

Lily left the room and went to the kitchen to prepare the evening meal. Mabel would need nourishing as well as the babies if she were to gain strength. Instead of the household becoming closer with the arrival of the babies, it seemed to be falling apart.

'You're looking worried again, Lily.' Samuel bounded into the kitchen. 'Now I am here you will cheer up.'

Lily was pleased to see him. 'Why is that?' she asked, breaking a smile.

'Because I have decided my next painting will be a scene with a happy person sitting in a garden.'

Lily thought about the painting propped up on the chest in her bedroom which she was going to send to her mum. It was a good likeness, but had a dream-like quality. 'You've only just finished the one of me for my mum. Now, I must get on, I've lots to do.'

'I want to paint a picture of a happy young woman and the only person I want to paint is you. Will you be happy for me?' Samuel sat down and sighed. He banged his fist on the table. 'That man has no right to steal the happiness from this house.'

He looked sad and Lily moved to be nearer him. 'Don't let Cecil upset you again. We all dislike him. Those poor little mites with him as a father. At least they have gentle Mabel and capable Eta to love them.'

'You're right.' He put out a hand and Lily grasped it, enjoying its soft warmth. Would they share another kiss? Samuel pulled her to him and they did. Only the thought of Cecil bellowing because dinner was late, made her break free. She stayed close to Samuel and inhaled the pungent oakmoss smell.

'I must get on with my work or Mr Potts will be after me.'

Samuel nodded and stood up. 'I shall see if Eta needs help and then I'll go to my room. I might write a poem. You inspire me, Lily.'

'Will you be at dinner?'

'I might be late.' He winked at her. 'In which case, I shall have to eat in the kitchen.'

As they were finishing their meal, Eta joined them and slumped in a chair. 'I don't blame you for having your meals here with Lily, I only wish I could too.

That man is unbearable. How we didn't see it when he first came here I cannot understand. I feel that life has become hard and dreary. Our only joy is the twins.'

'Let me fetch you a sherry from the parlour, Eta,' Samuel offered and made to leave the room.

'Bring one for yourself and Lily too.'

When they all held their glasses, Eta raised hers, 'To a better future.'

Lily almost choked when she took the first sip and Samuel patted her on the back and laughed.

'I never drink,' she said.

They enjoyed the company of each other in silence until Eta said, 'I've been saving money. Squirreling it away from the shop profits, just in case. With Mabel being unwell I wanted some money to fall back on to pay medical bills. I know Cecil won't help out with them. Even Mabel doesn't know about the savings and I don't want you to tell her.'

'Of course we won't. It was a thoughtful thing to do. I worry about you, Eta. I know in winter you don't have so much to do outside, but with spring coming you will be working in the garden in addition to the beer house, doing the accounts, ordering and seeing to deliveries. And then there are Mabel, Archie and Sylvan to see to. You do too much,' said Samuel.

'You make me feel even more tired, listing my jobs, but there is nothing else I can do except keep everything going as best I can. And with Bertha and Lily's help I'm sure we'll manage.'

Lily felt sorry for her mistress who looked worn down and miserable. Little pink patches on her cheeks had formed from drinking the sherry and her face was pinched. She'd lost weight and her hair was untidy.

'Yes, I'm sure we can manage if we all pull together,' Lily said.

'You do more than enough and even Samuel here, who pays to lodge with us and should do nothing, helps out. I saw you with Mabel and the twins earlier today, Samuel. You have a fine voice for lullabies. Now let us all get some sleep, we need to be rested and ready for tomorrow.'

Lily cleared the glasses and yawned. She would sleep well and hopefully dream of Samuel singing a love song to her.

# 8

About a week had passed since the evening she had shared with Eta and Samuel in the kitchen, and there seemed to be a new bond between the three of them. Lily could overhear Eta and Cecil talking in the hallway.

Cecil's voice was raised. 'I will not have money wasted on her. Tell Lily to make some chicken broth and tell Mabel to pull herself together and not be such a weakling. She has responsibilities to me and to the children. They too are nothing but a nuisance and expense.'

'I have my own money, Cecil. I will pay for the doctor to come and I will pay for any medicines she requires. She appears to have another infection. We are different. I love her and you do not. You probably never have.'

'Keep your nasty thoughts to yourself. My relationship with my wife is private, not for you to discuss.'

After the evening meal, Eta called Lily into the dining room. 'Thank you for fetching the doctor quickly, Lily. We must all be thankful that Mabel has been seen by him and the medicine prescribed should soon be taking effect. I hope that she will be well enough to celebrate her birthday later in the week.'

'She doesn't get a birthday this year,' Cecil announced.

'She will have a birthday. It is the twenty-eighth of February in four days so we will celebrate her birthday then.'

'Her birthday is the twenty-ninth so we won't celebrate it.' He smirked. 'It's a non-occasion and I'll be working.'

'We have always celebrated her birthday. We will cheer her up by having a small party in the bedroom if she is still too unwell to come downstairs.'

Cecil stood and as he left the room said, 'I'm going to one of the other beer houses in the village, the company is better.'

Eta looked close to tears. 'That man is simply unable to be kind to my dear sister.'

'We'll do our best to give her a nice birthday, won't we Lily?' Samuel asked.

'Yes, shall I bake a cake? And make some dainty sandwiches?'

'We must give her gifts too,' Samuel suggested.

Lily didn't think she had anything to give. The few flowers in the garden should be left for the graveyard. Somehow she'd have to think of something.

On the twenty-eighth, Cecil left the house early and Mabel managed to rest during the morning and seemed in good spirits by the afternoon. Lily carried plates of food and a tray of drinks up to her bedroom.

'Happy birthday, Mrs Potts.'

'I thought you'd all forgotten. No one has wished me a happy birthday, not even Eta.'

'That's because we wanted your celebration to be a surprise.'

'Will Cecil be joining us?' Mabel plucked at the bed clothes and her eyes flickered to the door.

94

'I don't think so, but Samuel is coming. He is busy wrapping your gift.'

'He's a lovely man.'

'Who are you talking about?' Samuel asked as he and Eta walked into the room. Each picked up a baby as they started to cry. 'The babies woke up just in time to join the party.'

'Four weeks, can you believe it, Mabel?' Eta asked.

'Hardly, it's all been like a dream.'

Samuel handed Mabel a parcel. She unwrapped a painting of the woods at the back of the house. 'It's beautiful, thank you. The colours are perfect. You are a talented young man. Very charming, caring and thoughtful. You'll make someone a good husband.'

On hearing her words, Lily kept her head down not daring to look at Samuel. If only he could be her husband one day.

Lily passed her the gift she had decided on. It was a cross stitch of a lily she had been working on for her mother. She had decided Mabel was in most need of it.

'It's delightful, Lily. And I see you've

made a beautiful cake.'

Lily thought it was a little lopsided.

'Mabel always bakes her own birthday cakes and is very good at it. It is a shame you get too tired now to do what you love, Mabel.' Eta pulled a chair up to be close to her sister.

It was a happy party and Lily felt at ease in the atmosphere without Cecil around. The babies were content and lay on the bed with Mabel. Samuel busied himself passing round the plates and glasses and wouldn't let any of the women help. He was always polite and respectful and she adored him for it.

The birthday party seemed to have relaxed everyone. Mabel was looking a bit better and Eta wasn't as forceful as she often could be. Lily was pleased to be in the room with everyone, especially Samuel.

'I think we should leave you to rest, Mabel,' said Eta when most of the food had been eaten. 'When Lily's cleared the room, I shall come back and help you with the feeding of the babies.'

'I can do it, Miss Stratford,' said Lily, not wanting to be thought lazy.

Eta smiled. 'I shall enjoy it. They're delightful and I like to be with them and Mabel.'

'Very well. Thank you for letting me stay for your party, Mrs Potts.'

'Your cake was delicious, Lily. Thank you all for your gifts and for not forgetting me.' Mabel's face had lost its frown lines.

Eta hugged her sister. 'We could never do that.'

Samuel insisted on helping Lily carry the things down to the kitchen, where he stayed with her while she washed the plates and glasses.

'The cross stitch you gave to Mabel is a masterpiece.'

Lily laughed. 'I'd hardly call it that. But I enjoyed making it. It was for my mum for Mothering Sunday. I won't be free to go home with all the extra work of Mabel not being well and the babies to look after.' She sighed. 'I don't mind working hard, but I miss home.'

'You could write a letter to your mother.'

Lily shook her head. 'No, I couldn't as I can't write well.'

Now he'd know how silly she was and despise her, but he just said, 'Then I can write it for you, if you'd like me to.'

With the kitchen clean and tidy, Lily sat at the table with Samuel, savouring his closeness.

'Tell me what you want to say,' he said, staring at the blank piece of paper in front of him.

'Dear Mum, I won't be able to come home for Mothering Sunday as one of the sisters got married and has twins now. They are sweet little babies and I have to help her look after them. Also she has been poorly so I am kept very busy.' She stopped, mesmerised by the words forming on the paper from Samuel's pen. 'Your writing is beautiful, I wish I could write like that.'

'I could help you improve your reading and writing.' Samuel looked up from the page and smiled at her. 'I'm sure

98

you'd learn very quickly.'

'I might.' If she and Samuel were to spend time together, she may well decide to learn slowly just to be with him longer. She giggled and when he asked her what was funny, she chose not to tell him.

'What else would you like to put in your letter?' Samuel had his pen poised again.

Lily bent over the paper and her hair brushed Samuel's face. She turned to him and said, 'I'd like to put . . . ' There was no time to say more as Samuel's lips met hers and Lily gave herself up to enjoying the experience.

Lily was happy to be improving her reading and writing with Samuel. It was something she'd never thought possible before. A whole new world was opening up to her, but best of all was her closeness to Samuel.

'Your reading is coming on well, Lily. Writing is a joy, too. As well as poems and the occasional letter, I write a daily diary.'

Lily wondered if she featured in his

diary at all. What would he say about her? Would he express any feelings of love towards her?

'I thought I might see if you can read some of my diary.' He grinned. 'What do you think?'

'I don't want to read anything private.'

'Do you think you might be mentioned?'

'I suppose I might. We do live in the same house and spend time together.'

Now that Samuel had mentioned it, Lily admitted to herself she was intrigued by what he wrote in his daily journal. She was keen to know what he'd said about her, if anything, and hoped she would be able to read the words.

'Here we are then.' He put a diary on the table in front of them and opened it at a page near the beginning.

'The tenth of January, eighteen-ninety-three.'

'Very good.'

'Today I fell in love with a ... I can't read this word,' Lily said.

'It's beautiful, but difficult to read.'

Lily continued. 'Beautiful maid called Lily.' She was overjoyed. He had fallen in love with her the day she had arrived at The Limes! 'I didn't know, Samuel.'

'Did you feel the same?'

'I did. I felt an attraction the minute I saw you.'

He held her hand, raised it to his lips to kiss. 'Let's not read any more. I have a plan.'

'I have to clean.'

'Lily, walk with me in the woods today.'

She sighed. 'You know I can't. I have the house to clean and then there are other jobs as always.' It would have been delightful to run into the woods with only Samuel for company, but it was not possible.

'Then come into the garden, just for a few minutes. There may be daffodils which you could pick to take to the churchyard. Mabel and Eta would like that.'

Lily smiled. 'What a good idea. Yes, I will come to the garden. But not for long.'

When they returned to the house, the babies were crying and Lily immediately felt guilty. 'I shouldn't have gone with you,' she said.

'You enjoyed it, though,' teased Samuel. She glanced at him and he kissed her cheek. 'Go on upstairs, I will put the flowers in the kitchen.'

Lily wasn't surprised to find him still in the kitchen when she returned after being told by Eta and Mabel she wasn't needed upstairs.

'You were quick,' he said, as he placed the vase of daffodils on the kitchen table. 'There, all ready to take over the lane to the grave when you get the chance. I will happily go with you.' He picked up his diary. 'Lately this has had some unhappy entries. Mr Potts has caused it. My poetry has been stunted by his arrival too.'

'Tell me some of your poetry,' she suggested.

He thought for a moment. 'Compare her to a summer rose, rather than a summer's day, once a bud with tenderness unfolding.' He stopped and smiled at her. 'I won't go on. It's about a girl.' Lily wondered if he meant her. 'I would like to share my paintings with you. Come on, let's go to my room.' He took her hand and laughing they ran up the stairs.

He removed a sheet from one of the paintings with a flourish. 'There. What do you think?'

The painting was of the church and churchyard and although it was painted in sombre colours there was a delicate simplicity to it. Lily didn't know what to say, but blurted out, 'I like the atmosphere. It isn't dead and dull. It looks like a place you could enjoy.'

'Perfect. I knew you'd see what I was trying to capture. Let me show you another.'

'I have to go, Samuel. I have things to do.'

'But the daffodils. Let's take them to the churchyard now.'

'Later. I must get my jobs done first.'

'Then please sit down a moment, Lily, I have something important to tell you.'

He gestured towards the bed. She sat down, wondering what he was about to say.

'I have been thinking a lot about the situation here. The atmosphere is off-putting and stifling, and my painting and writing are suffering, but I think you will be all right. Cecil doesn't take any notice of you. I imagine he sees you, being a maid, as beneath him so I am sure you won't have a problem with him except generally as we all do.'

Lily gulped. She longed to tell him that Cecil was very interested in her, but didn't know what Samuel's reaction would be.

'Knowing that you will be all right with Eta and Mabel, I have decided to leave. I will tell them this evening and move out as soon as possible. I have acquaintances in town I can stay with temporarily until I find another lodging place. I want to live simply without anything holding me back.'

Lily was distraught. How could he do this to her? Didn't he care about her one bit? And what about Eta and Mabel? They would be left to deal with Cecil alone. What would happen to them without Samuel to help and protect them?

105

# 9

Lily hadn't been able to speak when Samuel had told her his plan to leave The Limes and had rushed from his bedroom straight to hers. She stayed there as long as she could as she needed time to pull herself together.

After calming down, she thought more clearly about the problem. It was plain that Samuel didn't love her as much as she loved him. If he felt as strongly as she did he wouldn't be able to simply walk away and leave her to deal with Cecil without him. But the sisters needed him more than ever. There was something he didn't know which could change his mind. She decided to speak to him before he mentioned his plan to Eta and Mabel.

The cleaning and other tasks were particularly hard that morning, but when she'd finished, Lily knocked on Samuel's door.

'Come in.'

When she walked in he put down his palette and brush and gazed at her. 'I will miss you, Lily.'

'I don't think you will leave us,' she said.

'I am determined to go.'

'I have something to tell you which may change your mind. I don't suppose you realise how badly Eta and Mabel need your contribution to the household income. Mabel sees the doctor regularly and the medicine he prescribes is expensive. You do not know this, but Mabel isn't the only person who is unwell. Eta is suffering too. She is struggling and I am not sure how much longer she can keep the beer house and shop open, even with Bertha's help.'

'I had no idea, Lily.' Samuel moved to sit on his bed.

'She doesn't want anyone to know, but she has been having funny turns.'

'Dizziness?'

'Yes. She is often muddled. I think it's because she is too tired to think straight.

Mabel, who is growing weaker, says her sister is worn out. Of course, Cecil's unkindness to his wife is a great worry to Eta and I believe she doesn't sleep well. She is exhausted.

'If you stay, then at least Eta won't have to worry about money. As far as I can tell Cecil doesn't pay anything towards the cost of the household. Although, surprisingly, Bertha says he often buys Eta a drink when they're in the beer house together, and he still treats himself to smart clothes and goes out almost every evening. We need both you and your money.'

Samuel stood and took up his painting things again. 'Thank you for telling me, Lily. I will think about what you have told me and make my final decision this evening.'

Lily left the room feeling unhappy that he hadn't immediately agreed to stay. Surely the welfare of his friends, the women who had taken him in, was more important than his own feelings?

She was seeing a side of Samuel she hadn't been aware of before and it was one she didn't like.

She worried that he would still leave and, after the mid-day meal, she decided to take the daffodils to the Stratfords' grave. The joy of picking them with Samuel had gone and she felt sickened by their strong smell.

Once there she arranged the daffodils in the pot and pulled out a few weeds surrounding the headstone.

'Lily.'

She stood and wiped her dirty hands down the front of her skirt. 'Samuel.'

'I have come to apologise. I have been selfish and thoughtless. Eta and Mabel took me in and cared for me when I needed it most. Now I must care for them as best I can.'

'You'll stay?'

'I will.'

Lily couldn't help throwing herself into his arms and smothering his face in kisses.

He grinned. 'Hardly the right conduct for a churchyard, Lily. Let us hope Reverend Mason doesn't catch you.'

'I don't care. I am happier than I have been all morning. Let us sit on the wall for a few moments.' She didn't care who saw them.

It was a bright, sunny day and warm for March. Lily wouldn't have minded if it had been pouring with rain. Samuel may not have chosen to stay because he had strong feelings for her, but he had chosen to stay for his friends and she liked him better for that.

'I will keep an eye on Eta and also on Cecil. I have seen the way he behaves with women in the village and beer house. I have been thinking about what I said to you earlier. That he wouldn't be interested in you because you are a maid. I may be wrong. You are a very attractive young woman. I must protect you from any advances he might make.'

Lily lowered her eyes. She longed to share everything with Samuel, but this one thing she had to keep from him.

'I do believe though, that even if Eta is unwell, she is more than equal to Cecil.'

The next couple of months passed

peacefully enough and they all came to accept Cecil's unpleasant manner and learnt to deal with it, each in their own way. He was often out and Lily avoided him as much as possible. The health of her two mistresses was still a great worry to her and Samuel. They talked about it when he was giving her a lesson or when she was able to leave the house for walks with him.

Happily the two babies were healthy. Lily was singing to them in the kitchen as she moved their pram backwards and forwards in the hope that they would fall asleep. They were both grizzly.

A terrific crash from the shop made the babies jump and Lily hurried in to see what had happened. Eta was on the floor, the stepladder lying beside her. The customers were all talking at once and Lily had trouble thinking what to do. Rushing to Eta's side she saw a pool of blood seeping from under her head.

'We need to get her to bed and call the doctor.'

A large man stepped forward. 'I can

carry her. If you'll lead the way.'

'Someone fetch the doctor,' Lily ordered.

A woman called out, 'I'll go,' as she ran from the shop.

Samuel appeared. 'The babies are crying. What's going on? Eta? What's happened?'

'I'm going up with Eta,' Lily told him. 'Make sure the babies are all right. Take them in to Mabel and close the shop.' Lily was shaking and she wasn't sure if she'd make it up the stairs, but knowing she had to get Eta safely in bed she led the way.

The doctor arrived shortly afterwards along with Samuel. As the doctor examined Eta, Samuel grasped her hand and squeezed it. She could feel tears were coming and wiped her face with her hand. Eta was pale and unmoving.

'I'm afraid she's had a very nasty bang to the head. Not much we can do except see how things go over the next few hours. Sit with her and comfort her if she wakes. Does Mrs Potts know what's happened to her sister? Perhaps she should come and sit with her. You never know.'

With that Lily burst into tears and sobbed uncontrollably.

'Now, now, dear girl, Miss Stratford may well make a full recovery. Bumps to the head are unpredictable.'

'Sit here, Lily.' Samuel led her to an armchair by the window. 'I will let Mabel know what the doctor has said and she can bring the babies in. Their noises may comfort Eta so long as they are not wailing.'

'And I must go. I have another patient I need to visit. I will call later to see how Miss Stratford is getting on.'

Lily sat by the bed looking at Eta, who was lying as still as frozen snow and almost as pale. Her eyes were closed and her mouth slack and Lily was afraid for her. For once she was vulnerable and it was up to the rest of the household to care for her.

Samuel returned to the room and whispered that he'd shut the beer house and shop and Mabel would be in soon with the babies whom she was feeding and changing to keep them happy while they sat with Eta.

'I'll make tea for us when Mabel gets here, she's deeply upset by this accident.'

'We must make sure she's well looked after as well as Eta,' said Lily, worrying that she wouldn't be able to do what was needed. Then she remembered she had Samuel to help her. What would she do without him? But now was not the time to think about herself, she must concentrate on the household. Oh goodness, what would happen if Cecil came in? Don't think about it, she told herself.

Mabel walked unsteadily into the room, carrying the babies in her arms. Samuel immediately took Archie and Sylvan from her. Lily saw tears forming in her eyes as she stared at Eta in the bed. 'Sit here, Mrs Potts,' she said, softly.

Mabel slid into a chair and took a handkerchief from her pocket. She put a hand to her sister's face and stroked it gently. 'Wake up, Eta, it's Mabel and the babies. They are here with me. Please wake up.'

Lily could hardly bear to watch.

'She's not answering,' said Mabel, turning to Lily and Samuel. 'Why won't she speak to me?'

'The doctor said it might be a while before she responds,' said Samuel.

'Eta hasn't been well for a while, has she? I wonder if there's more to it than just having a dizzy spell and falling off the ladder,' said Mabel.

'What could it be? She's been run ragged with all the work she has to do. Not that it's anyone's fault,' Lily said, hoping Mabel hadn't taken offence.

'No, of course not, but Cecil hasn't helped at all, has he? Although sometimes he's taken me aback by taking a hot drink or a bowl of soup to Eta when she's been in the beer house.' Mabel shook her head and sniffed into a handkerchief.

Lily took the babies while Samuel went down to make tea. When he returned, he said, 'You must drink this, Mabel, it will make you better able to stay awake and comfort Eta.'

For the first time since entering the room, Mabel took her eyes from Eta and almost smiled at Samuel. 'Thank you. I will try to drink some.' She took the cup and put it to her lips.

Daylight turned to darkness and Eta stayed the same, still and unresponding. No one had any appetite for food, despite Lily trying to persuade Mabel to have something to eat for the sake of the babies. She shook her head and grasped Eta's hand, murmuring to her. 'I am here, Eta, I am by your side as always. Please wake up.'

Lily looked at Samuel who was now cradling the twins. He gave her a small smile and she said, 'Shall I take the babies? They probably need changing again by now.' She was pleased for an excuse to escape from the sick room. She fled to Mabel's room, slowing down when she remembered Cecil could possibly be in there. A knock on the door put her mind at rest and she entered an empty room. After changing the babies, she returned to Eta's room.

Samuel held out his hand for Sylvan, and Lily gave her to him. As she did so, Sylvan started to cry. Eta's eyes opened.

'Look,' said Mabel, 'She's woken up. Oh, Eta, you're better.' Eta seemed to gain strength and started to struggle upright. Mabel smiled at Lily and Samuel, 'She's going to be all right.'

Lily wasn't too sure it would be that simple a recovery, but she hoped it would be. 'Mabel,' said Eta, her voice quite clear. 'I heard the babies.'

'They're here,' said Mabel, and beckoned for Samuel and Lily to let Eta see them. Eta smiled and reached out for Mabel's hand. 'I love you, dear sister.' Then her body went limp and all of her breath left her body.

# 10

Everyone in the household was miserable and upset. All except Cecil who was more unbearable than usual. He tried to insist that the beer house and shop should re-open, but didn't offer to lend a hand.

'It's most unfair of you to expect Mabel to take on duties other than those of a mother,' said Samuel a few days after Eta's death. 'She's anxious and ill and she needs time to grieve.'

'And you are the lodger,' said Cecil. 'The shop will open.' Samuel slammed his fist on the table. 'The shop remains closed.'

Lily was shocked to see that Cecil didn't argue with him. Her admiration for Samuel grew to bursting point. She hurried off to reassure Mabel the shop would remain closed.

'Nevertheless, I want to be well enough to take over Eta's responsibilities and to make sure the children are provided for. Has Cecil gone out?'

'I heard the door slam, so I think so,' answered Lily.

'Then I'll stay here in my room with the babies for a while, Lily. Please could you bring some warm milk? Sylvan, Archie and I will share it.'

Lily still had her cleaning and cooking to do. As she worked, she wondered what the future would hold. Eta had kept Cecil in check for the most part, but might Mabel be scared into obeying her bully of a husband? Then she remembered Samuel standing up to Cecil. If only Cecil wasn't around, they might be able to go back to being a happy household.

The atmosphere remained tense over the next few days. Without Eta keeping an eye on him, Lily dreaded bumping into Cecil or him finding her alone, but to her relief he spent a lot of time out of the house. She wondered if he was working or if he had another woman elsewhere. She wouldn't be surprised.

After the evening meal, Mabel fetched Samuel and Lily from the kitchen to join her and Cecil in the dining room. Lily wondered if it was anything to do with the visit to The Limes of a smartly dressed man that morning. Mabel had been in the parlour with him for over an hour while Lily had cared for the babies.

'I'm going out,' Cecil announced.

'I shouldn't, if I were you,' Mabel said. 'This is a very important matter. I am going to tell you about Eta's will.'

Cecil immediately sat down. 'Get on with it.'

'Samuel, Lily, please take a seat, it is important you both know the situation.'

Samuel sat close to Lily and gave her a reassuring smile. She was worried that Mabel was going to give them some bad news. There had been enough of that already; first Cecil's arrival and then Eta's death.

Then she remembered the good things; the lovely man she had met who was now her friend and the two dear babies who constantly brought delight.

Her mum always told her to count her blessings and she would try to heed her words.

Cecil was thrumming his thighs with his fingers. 'I have things to do.'

Mabel sat down and picked up some papers. 'This is Eta's will.'

Cecil sat still and looked at his wife.

'My dear sister has left her half of the house and household goods to me, along with her personal possessions.'

'What else did you expect?' Cecil demanded 'She was hardly going to leave it all to the maid, was she?' he scoffed.

Mabel ignored him. 'I plan on re-opening the shop and beer house. Tomorrow. With the profits from there and with Samuel's rent we will be able to manage as before. However, Cecil, you have a good job and should be contributing to the finances. I am your wife and you now have two children to support. You need to remember the vows you made in church when we married. You must take on your responsibilities. In fact, I demand that you do.'

Lily was shocked that Mabel was standing up to Cecil. It was as though she had become stronger through Eta's spirit. Before Eta's death, Mabel had been too poorly to help in the house or the shop and now she seemed to have gained strength from somewhere.

'It's quite wrong,' Cecil growled. 'Women shouldn't be able to own property. Your husband should have control of the property and finances. The problem is you lack the brains, stamina and competitive drive to run a business.'

Samuel stood. 'Mabel is as capable as you. You are treating her cruelly and I will not have it.'

'She is my wife. It is nothing to do with you. I think we may well manage without a lodger from now on.'

Lily gasped. If Samuel was sent away she couldn't stand living at The Limes any longer. But she couldn't leave. Her family depended on her.

Cecil stood and walked closer to Mabel. 'We all know Eta was different. She was strong and clever. You are weak and silly. Looks as though I married the wrong woman.'

Lily could see that Mabel's hands were shaking and she longed to reach out and comfort her. Tears started to pour down her face.

'Typical! I suppose you think tears will make me sympathetic. Your tears and weakness don't work on me,' Cecil sneered.

Mabel wiped her face and took a deep breath. 'My tears are of frustration and anger at how manipulative and callous you have been throughout our marriage. My friend, protector and kindred soul is dead. Now I must have the strength to do what is best for the people I love.' She looked across at Lily and Samuel. 'And I have more to tell you. You will not like this one bit, Cecil, but my sister's will stipulates that in the event of my death, the share of the house and household goods Eta has left me will pass to Sylvan and Archie.'

'But they're babies!' Cecil's face was red and his eyes bulged.

'I do not intend on dying just yet, Cecil.

I hope to see them grow into adults.'

Lily was full of admiration for Mabel.

The next day Lily was working in the kitchen when there was a rap on the front door. She wiped her hands on her apron, smoothed her hair and went to answer it. When she saw Reverend Mason standing on the front step, she wondered what he had called for. Perhaps it was to see how Mabel was getting on and to offer her some Christian comfort. Then she thought that perhaps they had been neglecting the graves as they had been very busy. Mabel would be horrified if that was the reason for his visit.

'Good morning,' said Harold Mason. 'I've come to see Mr Potts.'

'Please come in, sir,' said Lily, opening the door wider in welcome, hoping nothing sinister was about to erupt.

While he waited in the hallway, Lily scurried to the beer house to find Mabel, who said Cecil was in the parlour and to invite Reverend Mason in to join him.

'Wasn't that Harold's bicycle I saw by

the front door?' asked Samuel, coming into the kitchen where Lily had retreated to continue preparing the meal.

'That's right, he wanted to speak to Cecil. He's in the parlour with him and Mabel now.'

'I wonder what he wants.'

'I don't know. But I would like to,' said Lily. 'I feel responsible for Mabel.'

Samuel nodded. 'I feel the same. Let's eavesdrop, shall we?' he said. He grabbed her hand and whisked her out of the back door and into the garden. He put his fingers to his lips.

They leant against the house wall and were able to hear what was being said through the open window of the parlour.

They heard the vicar's voice saying, 'I've been visited by a parishioner who has taken out a life assurance policy. He wanted to know more about it and wrote a letter to the company. It turns out that the policy does not exist. Not satisfied with that, the client investigated further and traced you, Mr Potts, back to The Limes.'

Lily pulled Samuel's head nearer to her and whispered, 'There you are, proof that he's a bad apple.'

'Not proof exactly, hearsay, more likely,' Samuel whispered back. She was sorry when he moved away from her to listen to more of the conversation coming from the parlour.

'I can assure you,' said Cecil, sounding pompous, 'Everything will be in order. What your parishioner probably doesn't realise is that there is a time lapse between the taking out of a policy and it being registered with the company. I explain things to people with great care, but they appear not to want to listen and are too ignorant to understand.'

'Are you sure that's what happened?' asked Mabel.

'You don't understand my work, Mabel, please don't bother yourself with it.'

'So you think he has nothing to worry about?' asked Reverend Mason.

Lily and Samuel heard a deep sigh from Cecil. 'If it puts your mind at rest,

I will make sure all is well. If you tell me the name of the man, I shall check his policy and make sure everything is in order. Does that satisfy you?'

'Yes, it does. And thank you very much for your trouble, Mr Potts.'

'Mabel will show you out,' Cecil said.

Lily and Samuel went back to the kitchen.

'Harold Mason sounded convinced, but I don't think I am,' said Lily. Samuel shook his head. 'No, not at all. It's all very suspicious.' 'What can we do?'

'I'll speak to Mabel, shall I, and see what she thinks about Cecil's honesty?'

'Yes please, Samuel. I'd feel much happier if you would.'

Despite Lily hoping things could be sorted out for the unfortunate client, the following week another visitor arrived at The Limes. He asked to speak to Cecil, who told Lily to say he couldn't see him as he had an important appointment in the town. The sly look on Cecil's face confirmed what Samuel had said after speaking to Mabel.

She had told him she wasn't sure her husband was honest.

'Tell him to come back another time,' were Cecil's parting words as he slipped out through the beer house door.

The man sighed and hung his head when Lily told him Cecil couldn't see him, but Mabel came to the door. 'What's it about?' she asked.

'An insurance policy,' he said. 'I'll come back.'

'No, it's all right. Now you're here, please come in. You look tired and hot. Perhaps a glass of beer would refresh you.'

'That would be welcome.'

'Lily, please bring it to the parlour.'

When Lily went to the parlour, Mabel said, 'Thank you, Lily. I wonder if you and Samuel would come in here and listen to what Mr Smith has to say.'

'Of course, Mrs Potts, I'll fetch Samuel.' Not only another chance to be with Samuel, but also more to be heard about Cecil's wicked goings on.

The four of them sat in the parlour and listened to Mr Smith. 'It was difficult for me to visit you, but in the end I had no choice.' He cleared his throat and fidgeted. 'My child died.'

Mabel inhaled sharply. 'What a dreadful thing to happen. I am so very sorry.'

'Thank you. Her funeral has had to be postponed as we have no money to pay for it.'

Lily and Samuel glanced at each other.

Mr Smith took a sip of his drink. 'I took out a penny policy from Mr Potts when the baby was born last year. My wife is suffering not only by the fact our baby is dead, but that she cannot be laid to rest. A pauper's funeral for our child will finish her. There won't even be a headstone.'

Mabel, Lily and Samuel had tears in their eyes as they looked at him. Lily felt very sorry for him and his wife. If Cecil were to blame, and she was sure he was, she'd like him to face some punishment for his actions.

'What brought you here?' asked Samuel.

'The insurance company said they had

no record of a policy. I live nearby and thought the vicar of the church might help me in tracing the person I bought the policy from.'

'And he sent you here?' asked Mabel.

Mr Smith nodded. 'Can you help me?'

'The person who sold you the policy is my husband. I will demand an answer from him!' Mabel's eyes glittered, but Lily knew that was from rage. 'Lily will see you out when you're ready to leave. I'm sorry I cannot give you any money, but we have none to spare.'

Mr Smith stood up. 'You've been more than kind, Mrs Potts. Thank you for seeing me.'

'I'll get in touch with you through Reverend Mason,' said Mabel.

Samuel opened the parlour door for Mabel to leave and then reached into his pocket and handed the man some coins. Lily had no idea how much he had given him or how much he could afford, but she was touched by the generous gesture.

After she'd shown Mr Smith out, Lily found herself experiencing feelings she had never felt before and was sure she was in love with the handsome, charming Samuel.

# 11

Tension mounted at The Limes and Lily felt as though the place would explode when Cecil came home. She prepared the evening meal as usual, but dropped several things and cut herself. It was late afternoon when she heard the front door open. She stopped what she was doing and took a deep breath.

It seemed that Mabel had been waiting for the return of her husband as almost immediately she was in the hallway speaking to him. 'Cecil, I need to talk to you.'

There was no reply. Mabel raised her voice. 'Did you hear me, Cecil? I said I need to talk to you.'

'Don't you shout at me. I heard you. You chatter too much, but go on then, let's get it over with. I want to go to the beer house. I've been working hard and a man needs relaxation when he gets home, not a nagging wife.'

'Come into the parlour with me,' she said.

'Didn't you hear me? I'm going to the beer house. Maybe Bertha will give me some comforting words. Other women are kind to me, Mabel, not you though.'

'As you wish, Cecil, we will have this conversation here in the hallway where Lily and Samuel, our maid and lodger, can hear us. That doesn't matter to me. Why didn't you speak to the man, Mr Smith, who called today? He was upset and needed reassurance that the policy exists and there would be a payment for his child's funeral.'

'I had an appointment. I said that. I have a business to run. I don't have time to waste on moaning clients. He's a troublemaker. I knew that from the moment I met him. I regret selling him the policy now.'

'But he's been told there's no policy. His child died, and he and his wife want to give the child a proper funeral. There is no record of the penny policy he took out and which he has been paying into.'

Mabel's voice was loud and strong. Lily was constantly taken by surprise by this different Mabel.

'Like I said he's a troublemaker. Just because his child has died he wants everyone to be sorry for him.'

'I am sorry for him. If either of our two died, I would want them to have a proper funeral, not have them end up in a pauper's grave. Is there some mistake? Has he been paying into a policy or not? Why does the company deny its existence? If you have taken money from that poor man and spent it on yourself, I will never forgive you. Cecil, answer me, what have you done?'

'What are you accusing me of? How dare you say I have been taking money for a policy which does not exist? You'll regret this. You don't understand the ins and outs of my work. Is that all? Have you finished with your complaining and questioning? Do I have your permission to leave?' Sarcasm dripped from his words. 'I have been put off going to the beer house with your accusations and nagging. I am going into the garden for some peace and quiet and a smoke of my pipe. I want no more of your irksome allegations.'

Mabel walked into the kitchen and sat at the table. 'You heard?'

'I'm sorry, I couldn't help but hear,' replied Lily.

'Good. My husband's behaviour is intolerable. I am not sure how much more I can take. Nor do I know how to deal with this situation. I have to help Mr Smith, I have to get to the truth. Look what Cecil has done to me.' She held out her hands which were shaking. 'And my heart is pounding as though it will burst.'

Lily was impressed by Mabel's determination, and the drive she had shown since Eta's death was enormous. 'You are a brave woman.' She continued peeling the carrots.

'Hardly brave. Foolish, maybe. Weak. Silly.' After a few moments Mabel said, 'I have decided what we must do.'

'We?' Lily asked. She was alarmed

135

that Mabel said we. She didn't want any trouble with Cecil. All she hoped to do was avoid trouble and get on with her work.

'Yes. We need proof of his dishonesty and I want to find it now. He is in the garden and the babies are sleeping in their pram out there. I will go out and keep an eye on him, pretending I am there for the babies. If he attempts to come in I will delay him by continuing the argument. Meantime you fetch Samuel and search through Cecil's things in our room. I need you to find some incriminating paperwork. Something which will prove he is up to no good.'

'I'm sorry, but I can't read very well.'

'I know that, but Samuel can. Just find papers and show them to Samuel. Go along now.' Mabel stood and made her way to the garden.

Lily wasn't at all happy. If Cecil came in and caught them going through his things she couldn't imagine what would happen. But when she knocked on Samuel's door and told him the plan he was keen to start the search.

'You can be mainly listening out to make sure Cecil doesn't catch us. But also look for papers or a notebook with a list of names and numbers. You can do that easily. If you think you've found something hand it to me and I'll read what it says.'

He almost seemed to be enjoying himself.

As they entered the room her heart hammered in her chest. Every noise startled her. Was Cecil coming up the stairs and about to catch them? Once, when she heard a creak and was sure Cecil would enter the room any moment, she grabbed Samuel's hand. He glanced at her and put his finger to his lips before briefly squeezing her hand and continuing with the search. Several times she hoped she'd found what they were looking for and handed it to him, but each time he shook his head.

Just when she felt they'd been in the room long enough and the search was fruitless, Samuel held up a notebook and whispered, 'I think this is it. It's a list of names and payments with dates. Listen, this last week Mr Mears paid two and sixpence, Mr Whitehead one shilling, Mr O'Brien tuppence. It goes on. Let's see if we can find Mr Smith.' He thumbed back through the pages.

Lily desperately wanted to leave the room. The consequences of being found there by Cecil were unthinkable.

'Aha, here we are,' said Samuel. 'Mr Smith one penny. He's made payments just as he said.'

'Samuel, please, can we go?'

'Yes, this is what we've been looking for.' He held up the notebook. 'Mabel can send this information to the insurance company and see if these policies exist or are fake. It's exactly the proof she needs. I'll copy the details and return the notebook as soon as I get the chance. We don't want Cecil to find it's missing.'

While they all waited for a reply from the insurance company, Lily was on tenterhooks. She went about her duties as usual and frequently asked Samuel if

Mabel had heard anything.

'We will have to be patient,' he said. 'It has only been a few days since Mabel sent the letter and a copy of the names of the policy holders. The insurance company will have to check their records.'

'But what about Mr Smith and his wife?' Lily hadn't been able to get the man's grief-stricken face out of her mind since his visit.

'I don't know what will happen, but I think you need a diversion.'

That made Lily smile. If ever there was a diversion for her, it was Samuel. She looked at his face, so familiar now, and loved what she saw.

'When you've served the meal, I shall come to the kitchen to eat with you. And I shall bring some books for you to read from.'

He left the kitchen and Lily heard him going upstairs.

It was a very warm August day and the kitchen was airless, even with the back door open. Lily didn't feel at all hungry, but she knew Mabel needed to eat. As she stirred the soup, she thought about the change in Mabel since Eta's death. That kind of strength and determination was good, but in one as weak and frail as Mabel had always been, Lily was frightened as to what might happen if she got another infection.

The soup was ready, and the tripe and onions were tender.

Lily took the food into the dining room and saw Mabel was there alone. Cecil must have had an appointment. Sometimes he arrived home for the midday meal, but not always.

'Thank you, Lily. I will try to eat something, but I really am not hungry.'

'It's the heat, Mrs Potts. Please try.'

Mabel smiled and picked up her soup spoon. 'Your cooking is always delicious, Lily. I will do my very best.'

Lily went back to the kitchen and found Samuel already there, seated at the table. She ladled out soup for them both and cut chunks of bread to go with it. When they'd finished the meal and Lily had cleared the dining room, she returned to the kitchen.

'Shall we make a start with the reading?' asked Samuel, opening a book.

Lily nodded and put her finger on the page, concentrating on sounding the letters as Samuel had taught her. Just as she was about to read aloud the first words of Little Red Riding Hood, Mabel opened the kitchen door, looking flustered.

'Lily, Samuel, the post has arrived. There is a letter from the insurance company.'

Samuel stood up. 'What does it say?'

'I haven't opened it yet. Please would you both come into the dining room with me and we will look at it together.'

Settled around the table, Mabel read the letter and passed it to Samuel.

'It is as we expected. The insurance policies listed in the notebook you found do not exist. That includes Mr Smith's policy. There is no trace of it.' Mabel's tiny fist rapped the table and her lips narrowed. 'I cannot express how upset I am for those clients. I am outraged at Cecil's involvement and his cold-heartedness. It is beyond my understanding how anyone

141

can behave as he has. And still is behaving. He must be stopped and he has to be punished for what he has done.'

Lily's mind was racing. Having taken in the fact that the policies did not exist, what rights would the clients have? She was also worried about Mabel who looked as though she might collapse due to her anger.

Samuel looked up from reading the letter. ' I am sorry you have this to deal with, Mabel.'

Mabel seemed to deflate and shook her head. 'How could he be so dishonest and swindle hard-working people as he has done? I just don't understand it.'

Lily knew she must do something as Mabel was now pale and shaking. 'Let me help you to your room, Mrs Potts. You need a rest.'

Without protesting Mabel allowed Lily to help her upstairs where she lay on top of the bed with the window open.

Lily returned downstairs and found Samuel still sitting looking at the letter. 'Is there nothing to be done?' she asked him.

He shook his head. 'Not unless Mabel can make Cecil give them their money back, but that's not likely.'

'He wouldn't do that,' agreed Lily.

'Come on, Lily. Let's go to the kitchen and continue reading. It will take your mind off insurance policies. I think we should be around when Cecil returns in case Mabel needs help.'

Mabel was back downstairs by the time Cecil returned home later in the afternoon. She had changed her dress and tidied her hair. Lily was asked to make tea which she took to the parlour. She left the room and heard Mabel say, 'Cecil, I got in touch with the insurance company who confirm you have been dishonest and the policies for which you have taken money do not exist. Would you like to explain that to me, please?'

Lily stayed in the hallway to listen to the conversation, telling herself she was there to protect Mabel if necessary.

'You know nothing about the matter,' said Cecil, a dismissive edge to his voice.

'Leave me to do my work and you get on with yours.'

'I am your wife, Cecil.'

'Unfortunately, yes you are, Mabel. Now leave me alone.'

'Not until you tell me what you are going to do about the policies.'

'They are none of your business,' shouted Cecil.

'And none of yours apparently, as they do not exist.'

Lily was upset at the argument she'd just heard and went to the kitchen, where she saw Samuel in the garden near the back door. She beckoned him inside and he came in pushing the pram.

'Mabel left the babies outside with me. They've been fast asleep.' Samuel put his arm round her and held her gently. 'It will all turn out all right, Lily.'

'How will it? That poor man and his wife won't have enough money for the funeral now. And what about the other people who have been giving him money?'

'I don't know, but it is not your concern. You didn't steal the money from them. You are a gentle, caring soul and I hope you remain that way.'

One of the babies was making whimpering sounds and almost immediately the other joined in. Lily was reluctant to be separated from Samuel as she was enjoying his closeness, but she picked Archie up and Samuel took Sylvan. They sat on chairs side by side and cuddled the children.

'What will become of these poor babies? I love them very much and can't bear the thought that they will have to spend their lives with that awful man.' Lily kissed the top of Archie's head.

'They have a loving mother and they have us. The three of us can make sure they lead happy and fulfilling lives.' Samuel bounced Sylvan up and down on his lap.

'Can we? How? Cecil will be unkind to them, just as he is to Mabel. And which of us will be able to stop him? They are innocent and, if the truth comes out, will be tarnished by their father's dishonest actions. What will happen? Will the insurance company inform the police? Will he go to jail?'

Samuel put a hand on Lily's arm and stroked it lightly. 'Lily, Lily, calm down. You ask too many questions and I do not have the answer to one of them. We must wait and see. Look Sylvan has fallen asleep again.'

He stood and put the baby back in the pram before rocking it gently.

'Archie is taking a little longer, but I think if I put him in with Sylvan he will soon join her. Are you going to carry on rocking them? If so, I can get on with my work.'

After a short while Samuel put his finger to his lips and whispered, 'They are both asleep now. Please take two minutes to sit with me. Your work can wait.'

Once seated, Samuel took her hand. 'I am inspired by you. I have written another poem and when it's polished I will read it to you. Only the best is good enough for a fine girl like you.'

The bad feelings of the day disappeared. Lily was elated by his attention and words. Her greatest wish was to have more cosy times like this with Samuel.

Lily managed to avoid Cecil for the next few days, and was alarmed when he found her in the kitchen.

'The pretty young maid. And all alone. Come here,' he said.

'No, sir, I will not. I have work to do. I want to bake some chicken pies for tomorrow.' She was making pastry and held up her floury hands.

'It can wait. That invalid of a wife of mine eats like a sparrow.' He leered at her.

Lily wasn't sure who was in the house. She'd seen Samuel go out after eating earlier, but had he returned? Mabel was upstairs with the children and even if she came down it was possible she wouldn't be able to help at all.

She would have to deal with Cecil on her own.

Unable to keep quiet any longer, she blurted out, 'You're a wicked man and Mabel was unfortunate to be taken in by your false charms. You have cheated hard working people and you have ignored those you should love. You should treasure Mabel, she is a good and kind woman and yet you treat her badly.'

'I like your fire. It is exciting.' He sat down. 'Come and sit on my knee.'

'Leave me alone. I dislike you more than you can imagine. I will not willingly come to you.'

'Then I must come to you.'

He stood and moved towards her, grabbing her by the waist and ripping off her apron. His face came close to hers and she wanted to scream, but her fear was too great for her to do anything. She smelt the sour breath from his mouth as he tried to kiss her and she squirmed out of his grasp. He grabbed her head and pulled her face towards his.

'Get off me!' she said. 'You are drunk. I can smell it on your breath.'

She pushed at him and he let her go. In spite of being unsteady, he managed to block her way to the door. He lunged at her again and, with his arms round her, they swayed.

'Dancing, I like dancing.'

'Let me go!'

As she said the words she was aware of another person in the room. Samuel was there to rescue her.

'Leave her and get out of this house for good!'

Cecil let her go. 'You can have her. I've got all I can from this family. I thought there would be more pickings. They gave me respectability for a while, that was all. I'll be pleased to leave this wretched and dismal household.'

Samuel made a move towards him, jabbing a finger at him and scowling. 'If you don't leave now I will contact the police and tell them how you cheated people. I said get out, now move!'

Cecil turned quickly and lost his balance. He fell heavily, banging his head on the range. Lily stumbled to Samuel and fell in his arms.

'Come, Lily, let us leave the kitchen until this scoundrel has gone.' He turned in the direction of Cecil. 'You had better be gone by the time I get back. And when

Mabel hears about your latest wickedness she will want nothing more to do with you.'

Cecil moaned.

Samuel led Lily into the parlour and sat her down in an armchair. He poured some brandy and handed it to her. 'I think you should drink this. It will help you get over the shock you've been through. I am sorry I didn't arrive earlier. Poor Lily.'

Lily sipped the drink he offered and, as the powerful spirit entered her body, she began to relax. She lay her head on Samuel's arm and he stroked her hair.

'It's all right, Lily. I'm here. You'll be all right. We'll stay here as long as you like until you feel better.'

If Samuel was beside her all the time, she would be very happy. She closed her eyes, but saw Cecil's cruel face so opened them again. 'I wonder if he's gone,' she said.

'I'm not leaving you on your own until you've got over the shock. Then I'll go and see.'

Lily thought there might be another clash between the two and was worried.

When eventually Samuel left the room to check on Cecil, he was back very soon. 'There's no sign of him,' he said, holding Lily's hand.

'We must tell Mabel,' she said.

'We'll go together to tell her, but let's stay here a little longer shall we? I was going to say you need more time to get over your shock, but truthfully, I am enjoying spending the time with you.'

'Will we have to tell Mabel why he's gone? I mean about him molesting me? She might think I encouraged him.'

'I'm sure she won't, Lily. She's seen what he's like when other women are around and there's been talk in the shop which she must have overheard at some time.'

Lily lay back in the chair, letting Samuel hold her hand. They remained there quietly until Samuel said, 'If you're ready, shall we go and tell Mabel?' He helped Lily out of the chair and they went upstairs together.

Samuel knocked on the door, gently at first, but then, getting no reply, a little harder. There was still no reply.

'Perhaps she's asleep,' said Lily, covering a yawn. 'She's been very tired and overdoing things with looking after the twins and all the other work.'

'You're right,' said Samuel. 'Let's leave her to rest and break the news to her in the morning.'

'I must clean the kitchen and there are still the pies to make,' said Lily, suddenly remembering her half-finished task.

'The only one who would notice is Cecil and he's not here,' smiled Samuel. 'Why don't you go to bed and we can deal with the kitchen together in the morning.'

Crossing the landing and going into her room, Lily was already looking forward to the morning when she'd be spending more time with Samuel. Then she remembered the vile incident with Cecil and the fact they had to break the news to Mabel that her husband had left the house — and the reason why.

Lily slept fitfully and was relieved when morning came so she could fill her mind with something other than Cecil's behaviour.

When she reached the kitchen, she found Samuel was already there.

'Good morning, Lily. Did you sleep well? And are you feeling better this morning?'

'I'm fine,' she said, not wanting to dwell on the events of the previous evening. Then she realised she would have to as they had yet to tell Mabel her husband had left.

'Can I get you something to eat?' she asked.

'No, I've made some tea and now you're here, I'll pour you a cup.'

'Thank you, but I must clean the kitchen. What a mess. I hate leaving things like that.'

Lily looked around at the congealed dough in the dish and the flour on the table and over the floor. Then she glanced at the range and the patches of blood on the floor next to it. Cecil must have hurt

153

himself badly to have bled that much.

'You drink your tea and I shall clean,' said Samuel, pulling out a chair for her and placing it near the window. 'It's a beautiful day and you can enjoy the view of the garden.'

Lily would rather have enjoyed the view of Samuel, but she didn't say so.

'You're very kind, Samuel. Thank you, but I must get breakfast ready because Mabel will be in the dining room soon. I haven't heard the babies crying, have you?'

'I heard them some time in the night, so perhaps Mabel settled them and they went back to sleep.'

Lily stood up. 'I'd like to speak to Mabel as soon as we can, it feels like a millstone about my neck.'

'Very well,' said Samuel, 'Let's go to her room now, shall we? Is the tea still hot?'

Lily felt the pot. 'It is.' She reached for a cup and saucer.

When they reached Mabel's bedroom door, Samuel knocked.

'Come in, Lily,' said Mabel.

'Good morning, Mrs Potts,' said Lily, entering the room. 'Samuel's with me, may he come in, please?'

Mabel nodded. 'I'm not properly dressed, but I have a robe you can help me with, Lily. And would you look after the twins, I haven't changed them since the middle of the night.'

After putting down a cup of tea for Mabel, Lily began the task of changing the babies. Mabel looked exhausted and Lily was frightened as to how their news would affect her. Before either she or Samuel had a chance to recount the events of the previous evening, Mabel said, 'I think Cecil must have left for some reason.'

Lily and Samuel stared at each other.

Mabel continued, 'His things have gone. The wardrobe is empty of his clothes.'

'We have something serious to tell you, Mrs Potts.' Lily looked from Mabel to Samuel, who nodded and she continued, 'Mr Potts left the house last evening.

We do not think he will be coming back.'

Mabel went over to pick up Archie who had started to whimper. She cradled him and then asked, 'Do you know where he's gone, or why?'

'I told him he must leave,' said Samuel.

Lily held her breath as she waited for Mabel to be annoyed that he, the lodger, had done such a thing, but she said nothing immediately.

Mabel looked terrible; her face was pale and her eyes red. 'Why?'

Then Lily quickly told Mabel what Cecil had done to her.

Mabel gave Archie to Samuel and put an arm around Lily. 'That's a disgusting thing for any man to do! I am really sorry that you have had to put up with his nasty behaviour.' She hugged Lily lightly. 'Shall we all go downstairs and have some breakfast? I'm not hungry, but I know you like to feed me up.'

Lily was shocked at Mabel's reaction to Cecil's departure. She seemed relieved and not at all troubled her husband had left the household.

To Lily's surprise, Mabel followed her and Samuel into the kitchen. 'Shall I bring breakfast to the dining room?' Lily asked.

'Yes, in a moment. I think it's a good thing Cecil has gone, especially after what you say he did.'

'He didn't seem to make you happy after your marriage,' said Samuel, and Mabel nodded in silent agreement.

Then she looked over at the range where Cecil hit his head. 'Is that where it happened?'

'Yes,' said Lily. 'I shall clean it today, of course. And the stone flags where those blood patches are.'

'All the blood must go,' said Mabel, going over to inspect the spot carefully. 'In fact, I shall do the cleaning myself. In a way, I feel responsible for what happened to you, Lily,' she said.

The three had a meagre breakfast of tea and eggs, Mabel taking hers in the dining room, before joining them again. Samuel said he was going out to the woods later if the two women didn't need him. He added Cecil wouldn't be in any fit state to return to the house after his injury the previous night.

'I'll start at the top of the house,' said Lily, collecting her cleaning things after clearing the breakfast crockery.

If Mabel heard her, she gave no sign as she was already busy scrubbing at the dark stain on the floor.

When Lily returned to the kitchen some time later, Mabel was on her knees scrubbing the floor at the other side of the kitchen to the range. The paint on the wall above her looked damp too as though it had been wiped with a wet cloth.

'I noticed a stain here so thought I'd clean it up while I had a bucket of water,' Mabel explained.

'I'm sorry, I should have seen to that. I only washed the floor yesterday and it was spotless.'

'With us all coming in and out it's bound to get dirty quickly.' Mabel stood up.

'Let me empty the water out,' Lily offered.

'No, no. I will do it.'

When Samuel returned, Mabel had gone to see to the twins and Lily was sitting in a chair wondering whether or not to tell him how strange Mabel had been.

'What is it, Lily? You look as though you are in another place. That man, Cecil, has a lot to answer for.'

He pulled a chair up to be next to her.

'It was Mabel I was thinking of. She was behaving very strangely. Not only did she clean the blood off the range, but she cleaned something off the wall and floor over there. What could it have been?'

'Food? Mud from our shoes?'

'But why would she clean it up? And why did she want to clean the range? She was exhausted and yet insisted on doing it. She wouldn't even let me carry the bucket to tip the dirty water out. You don't suppose . . . no I'm sure my mind is confused because of Cecil's behaviour yesterday.'

'What are you thinking?' Samuel took her hands in his.

'I think she was cleaning up more blood. But he fell against the range. Why was there blood on the opposite side of the room?'

'Your thoughts are wild. He could have staggered over there and fallen again. Or maybe he crawled around for a while. I expect he had a bad head. He hit the range with some force.'

'I suppose you are right. But if his head wound has bled a lot, he could be very badly injured.'

After the discussion with Samuel about Cecil's injury, Lily felt uneasy. What he'd done was wicked, but she didn't like to think of him lying in a ditch somewhere without any help if his injury was worse than she and Samuel had at first thought. Then she wondered if he had recovered completely and sobered up.

'Samuel, I think there is every possibility he might come back and try to get his revenge.'

# 12

Lily's biggest fear was unrealised when Cecil made no appearance that night. She relaxed a little, hoping he really had left the house for good. With that thought in mind, she slept well.

It had been agreed when the twins were born that they would sometimes sleep with Lily to give Mabel more rest and also so as not to irritate Cecil. Lily found their company comforting and didn't mind when they woke during the night requiring attention.

That morning, when Lily got up to attend to her jobs, they were lying together peacefully. She paused to look at them. They were facing each other in the cot, their little fists curled. Archie had a smile on his face and Sylvan appeared to be pouting. For a moment, she wondered what they would be like as they grew up. Then she pulled on her uniform and went downstairs to the kitchen, knowing Mabel would fetch them if they became unhappy.

The sun was shining after the rain the previous day and Lily sang quietly as she prepared breakfast. It would be nice to see Samuel again and she hoped he wouldn't go out before they'd spoken. Sometimes, Lily made a small picnic for Samuel to take along with him, which she enjoyed doing and he said she made the most exquisite salted tongue sandwiches.

The babies started crying and interrupted her thoughts. She hurried up the stairs, before remembering that Cecil was the only person to complain when they cried. Mabel and Samuel were tolerant and enjoyed them being around.

'The children are awake, Mrs Potts,' said Lily, taking them into Mabel's room.

'I heard,' she said. 'I adore to see them.' She held out her arms and Lily placed them both on the bed beside their mother. Mabel made an extraordinarily attentive and loving parent.

Briefly, Lily thought of her own

mother, missing her very much. Then she gave her attention to Mabel, helping her feed and dress the children, the four of them enjoying the process that morning instead of having to quieten and hurry them into their clothes.

What a difference it made not to have Cecil in the house. It was as if Mabel sensed what Lily was thinking.

'I'm pleased Cecil's gone. I feel ashamed to say it as he was — is, my husband and the father of my children.' She looked at Lily. 'I know he wasn't popular with dear Eta, Samuel or you, but I thought I'd done well to find a husband.' Tears clouded her eyes. 'I should have known I didn't deserve to have one.' She brushed her eyes with her fingers, 'Pride comes before a fall, isn't that what they say?'

'We'll have to ask Reverend Mason,' said Lily, trying to ease the atmosphere. 'You have two beautiful children who are very lucky to have you as their mother.'

Mabel's cheeks flushed and she smiled at the children. 'They are delightful, aren't they?'

'Will you be coming downstairs for breakfast?' Lily asked.

Mabel shook her head. 'No, I shall stay in my room with the children.'

'Then I'll bring something up for you.'

'I'm very tired, Lily. I shall sleep.'

'Very well, Mrs Potts,' said Lily, disappointed that Mabel felt she had to rest as recently she'd seemed more invigorated than usual. However, she accepted what her mistress said. 'I'll take these things to wash,' she said, gathering garments from Mabel's room. 'And I'll come and clean your room and make the bed when you're ready. I shall listen out for Archie and Sylvan.'

'Thank you, Lily. You are one addition to the household who is an asset, as is Samuel.'

Lily went downstairs thinking of Samuel. There was no sign of him and she was unsure what to do about breakfast. She fried some kidneys and sliced some bread, which she ate with a cup of tea, leaving some in case Samuel appeared.

The next job, she decided, was the washing which could then be hung out in the sunshine to dry while she carried on with the endless task of cleaning. As she started to soak Mabel's clothes, she noticed mud on the hem of the skirt she had been wearing two days previously. Lily thought it very odd, as Mabel had not been outside at all as she'd been busy either serving in the shop or looking after her children. Deciding it was nothing to do with her, she carried on with her housework.

With the clothes drying in the garden and the downstairs rooms neat and clean, Lily was pleased with her progress that morning.

'Lily, would you look after the children now as I am going through to serve in the shop,' Mabel said, coming into the kitchen.

'Of course, Mrs Potts, but you haven't eaten anything today. Let me get you something, at least some bread and tea.'

'Very well,' smiled Mabel, 'I will give in, but just bread and tea. Although, truly, I have no appetite. I shall sit here with you in the kitchen.'

'Well, I have an appetite.' Samuel came striding in through the back door. Lily was very pleased to see him and told him there were some kidneys left from breakfast. Samuel smiled at her and sat at the table.

Lily sipped her tea, but it wasn't long before Mabel got up from the table. She swayed a little and had to steady herself by leaning on the wall.

Samuel bounded out of his chair and was at her side. 'Take care, Mabel. Come and sit down. You should rest. I can serve in the shop while Lily looks after the babies.'

'Perhaps you're right, Samuel,' said Mabel, looking pale and shaky.

'I will help you to your room, Mrs Potts, and bring the babies down. I can take them for a walk and when they wake up, we can play together. I shall enjoy being with them,' Lily said.

'You are both a blessing. Thank you.'

After Mabel was settled in her bed,

Lily took the babies downstairs and found Samuel was still in the kitchen.

'How is she?' he asked.

'She seems exhausted. It is such a disappointment as she has been so well recently. She is anxious and upset about something.'

'It's not surprising. Her husband has left. I imagine that has had a great effect on her.'

'Maybe, but she seemed pleased he'd left. I think her behaviour is strange. Her insistence on cleaning the blood herself. Wouldn't any other mistress have told the maid to do it? What do you make of that?'

'I haven't thought about it.'

Lily felt there was something odd going on at The Limes.

She loved being with the twins and couldn't help wondering what it would be like if they were her own children. It was very tiring being a mother, she decided, but Mabel had the added problem of being unwell. Once she'd finished her work, Lily thought about how she could make things more pleasant for her mistress. She decided to pick some flowers for her bedroom.

In the shed was a trug and an old knife. The first thing to take her attention when she opened the shed door was Cecil's suitcase.

How had it come to be there? Why was it there? Without stopping to think, she opened the case and inside were his belongings, clothes and personal washing and shaving items.

Brie.y, Lily wondered if Mabel was responsible for putting the suitcase in the shed. But for what purpose? If Cecil had gone away, he would have needed his things and there was no reason for him not to take them — unless he hadn't gone away after all.

In spite of the heat of the day, Lily shivered as she thought about Cecil being nearby. Then another thought crept into her mind: had Mabel possibly killed Cecil?

It was nonsense, Lily told herself. Picking up what she'd entered the shed for, she went into the garden and cut some of the pretty flowers.

When she got back into the house, Samuel was in the hallway. 'Bertha is in the shop and I've come to see how Mabel is now.'

'I've been picking flowers and I will take them upstairs to Mabel. I hope they will cheer her up.'

'They're pretty. You've arranged the posy well.'

'Samuel, while I was in the shed, I found Cecil's suitcase. Why do you think it was there?'

'I have no idea at all. Perhaps it was too heavy for him to carry on his way. He had his bicycle, of course, and that appears to be gone.'

'You think he's going to return for his suitcase?' Lily was horrified.

'I don't know, Lily. Please don't be afraid. He won't come back. He could easily have bought new clothes. You really mustn't worry about things so much.'

'I have another idea, Samuel, which I would like to tell you.' Lily took a deep breath, hoping Samuel wouldn't laugh at her. 'I was wondering if Mabel might have injured him or . . . or possibly even killed him.'

Samuel laughed loudly. 'Oh, Lily, please be sensible. Of course Mabel hasn't killed him! Can you picture her raising anything more than her voice to Cecil? Or to anyone. Don't forget she's very frail and incapable of doing anything like you are describing.'

Now Samuel had put things in proportion, Lily calmed down. 'I expect you're right. And Cecil is a strong man.'

'I think you should leave well alone and not speak of this to Mabel. We are better off without him, however he's left.'

Even though Cecil had left, things had changed since Lily's arrival at The Limes. It wasn't simply Eta's death and the birth of the twins. Now there was a new strangeness about Mabel. Lily had little time to dwell on it as she was busier than ever before.

'You look tired, Lily,' Samuel said as he joined her for breakfast as seemed to have become his habit now.

'I am. The babies were awake a lot in the night. I also heard Mabel shouting in the early hours of the morning. When I went in she was thrashing about having a nightmare. She's been doing that these last few nights. Haven't you heard her?'

'I sleep soundly. Must be all the fresh air I get.' He paused and then tucked into his breakfast of devilled kidneys.

'What is it, Samuel?'

'Nothing.'

'We mustn't have secrets, not after everything that has happened here.'

Samuel frowned. 'I didn't want to worry you. When I mentioned fresh air it reminded me that on my outing yesterday I found Cecil's bicycle abandoned in a hedge.'

'Where?' Lily could barely speak.

'Just beyond the house. Not far at all.'

'Why? Why would he leave it there?'

'Maybe it was damaged.'

'Or maybe we are meant to think that he left on his bicycle.'

'Lily, you must stop this daft idea that

171

he didn't leave of his own free will. We should celebrate that he is gone.'

Lily pushed her plate away. 'I am worried about Mabel. She is acting strangely.'

'It isn't surprising. The poor woman has had to put up with marriage to Cecil. That would drive anyone quite mad. I expect the relief of his departure has overwhelmed her.'

'What's that noise? I thought I heard the back door in the hall closing.' Lily felt bothered in spite of Samuel being there to protect her.

'I didn't hear anything. Apart from the nightmares, how is Mabel acting strangely?'

'She was active and almost healthy before Cecil left. Eta's death appeared to have given her the will to look after the babies and make sure the family was all right financially. But since Cecil left she has gone downhill. She doesn't seem to have any strength and hardly eats.'

'Mabel is bound to have relapses as she has never had a strong constitution. Does anything else worry you?'

'Her secretiveness. Before we would talk about all sorts of things and now she keeps everything to herself. We no longer have friendly chats where we might discuss anything.'

Samuel grinned. 'Including the very handsome lodger? I don't want to think about Mabel and her difficulties. I want to think about you. I long to spend more time with you, with no one to disturb us. To be relaxed and carefree. Getting to know you better is my dream.'

Lily was shocked Samuel apparently didn't care about Mabel, but was pleased he was thinking about her in that way.

'Samuel, don't you care about my mistress? I'm surprised at your lack of feeling. She has no one but us to support her.'

Samuel rubbed his cheek. 'It is true and I apologise for being selfish. I am sorry Mabel is unwell and because of that you have extra work. Is there anything else I should know?'

'Mabel has said several times she is not long for this world.' Lily suppressed a sob.

'Come, Lily, let us take a stroll down the garden and get some fresh air. It may help you feel better.'

He stood and held his arm out to her which she clasped, enjoying the feel of his skin.

As soon as they entered the garden they saw Mabel staring into the distance and taking no notice of the twins who she had put on the grass. 'I told you I heard the noise of a door. Mabel must have come down with the babies and through the back door of the hallway,' Lily whispered. 'How did she manage them both? Look at Archie, lying contentedly on his back gazing at the clouds and the sky. Where is Sylvan?'

Samuel darted away from her and down the garden to the rough bit where there were weeds and brambles. He scooped Sylvan up just as she was about to crawl into a patch of nettles.

The movement had caught Mabel's attention. 'What's happened? Oh, Sylvan! Oh, what have I done?'

'It's all right, Mabel. She is crying because I startled her when I took hold of her. Here, she needs you, her mother.' Samuel held the child out to Mabel.

'No, I can't take her. I am not fit to be her mother and care for her. The poor children! What have I done?'

Lily moved to Mabel's side and put her arm round her. 'You have done nothing wrong. You are unwell. Children can't be watched all the time. They will get into scrapes.'

'It's true, I am not well. I cannot care for my children as I should.'

'You are a good mother. Once you get strong and are well again, you will be able to do everything you want to do for them. It has been a trying time, but you are free from Cecil's unkindness as are the children. Your life will be better by far.'

Samuel hugged Sylvan to him.

'Will it? I need to provide for the children. I think we should sell the house and move. Get away from here.' She waved her hand around to include the house and garden. 'The memories are bad here and I don't want the children to grow up with that.'

'But this has been your home since you were born. It wouldn't be easy for you to move. Think about this thoroughly before you make a decision,' Samuel begged her.

'I have been thinking about it. I want to sell the house. I need the money to make sure the twins are provided for. I want you two to start preparing for the sale as soon as possible.

'Look through the house and see what we no longer need. See what is in the attic, clear it and get rid of surplus items before we move. We might be able to make some money by selling things. No one has been up there for years.' Mabel twisted her hands together.

'Are you sure about this, Mrs Potts?' Lily asked anxiously.

'I am quite sure. Everything needs to be in order. I shall die soon.'

'What do you think we should do about the clearing of the house?' asked Lily the following morning as she was hanging out washing and Samuel was handing the clothing to her.

'Mabel said to do it soon, but I'm not convinced she's serious about it. I think we should wait a few days at the very least,' replied Samuel. 'You have other ideas, don't you?'

'I feel that if she's got moving on her mind, she won't rest until it's done. At least we can clear the house and then she'll feel we've made a start.'

As she spoke, Mabel came into the garden. 'Lily, why aren't you clearing through the house? I thought I asked you and Samuel to help me.'

As she spoke, she paced up and down, her movements slow, her breath rasping.

'Mabel, it's all right. Please don't worry. Things will sort themselves out,' said Samuel.

'I want you to sort things out, Samuel. Please do as I ask you. Please help me.'

The effort of speaking seemed to wear her out and if Lily hadn't rushed to her side and steadied her, Mabel would have fallen to the ground.

Over Mabel's head, Lily looked at Samuel, her eyebrows raised trying to indicate to him that it would be a good idea if they told Mabel they'd do as she asked.

He nodded.

'Samuel and I were talking about that,' said Lily. 'We will go up into the attic and down into the cellar as soon as we've all eaten. I've almost finished here, as you can see, so you and Samuel go inside.' Feeling as if she were ordering her mistress around, Lily added, 'If that's all right with you, Mrs Potts.'

Mabel nodded and let Samuel help her into the house.

Lily quickly finished her job and then scooted to the kitchen to serve the liver and vegetables, which she'd prepared earlier that morning. She was pleased to notice that Samuel and Mabel were both in the dining room. Although she would have liked nothing better than to have had more time with him, she understood Samuel's reasoning for staying with Mabel.

He never ceased to impress her with his thoughtful ways.

When Lily was clearing the dining room at the end of the meal, Mabel said, 'I will go to my bedroom and stay with the children. Samuel and you, Lily, will start going through the house.'

'Yes, Mrs Potts,' said Lily, relieved things were finally getting underway. Hopefully, it would make Mabel feel better.

When they'd climbed the steep, narrow stairs to the attic Lily looked around, imagining what it would be like to sleep there. When she'd first arrived at The Limes she'd thought she'd be given an attic bedroom, not the best room in the house. It had seemed very strange to her, but she'd accepted Eta's explanation for giving her their parents' bedroom and it was better than this fusty attic room. Although Lily liked the quirkiness of the low beams and sloping ceiling, she was glad she didn't have to negotiate them each day.

'What a lot of things,' said Samuel, looking around. 'Some of them belonged to Eta and Mabel's parents I expect.'

Lily felt overwhelmed by the task, but she was close to Samuel, which didn't make it all bad. 'I've no idea what we're looking for, have you?' she asked.

'No, let'ssee exactly what there is.' He started turning random things over in the middle of the crowded space.

'No, not like that, it has to be more orderly,' said Lily, used to cleaning methods. 'We'll start in that corner and work our way around the room.'

Half an hour later, there were items in piles, and Lily felt they were getting on. One of the piles was things to keep and one was things to get rid of. She moved to the next area they were to sort.

'Oh, this box is heavy!'

Samuel was by her side hauling it away from the wall. He opened it and peered inside.

'Goodness me! This looks as if it might be something worth keeping.'

Lily leant over his shoulder and looked. 'Silver? Is that real silver? Mabel and Eta wouldn't have forgotten that

180

was up here, would they? They've always said they needed money and that looks as if it might be worth a lot. But I don't know if it is.'

Samuel pulled out the items and they both gasped. Lily fell back on the floor surrounded by the silver: a tea service, candlesticks, a cruet set, napkin rings, spoons and other items of cutlery. 'Well, I'm not going to look in the cellar now!'

Samuel laughed. 'I don't think it will be necessary immediately, no.' He sat down beside her, pushing a stray lock of hair from her face. 'Dear Lily. I love being with you. I knew I was doing the right thing moving in with the Stratford sisters. They were good to me and showed me a lot of kindness. Also, they encouraged me with my paintings. But the best thing is, they brought you to their house — and to me.'

Lily sniffed. 'Sometimes, I wish I had never come.' She reached for Samuel's hand. 'But I like being with you too. You have made the difficulties we have had with Cecil bearable.

'When shall we tell Mabel?' asked Samuel.

'Straight away,' said Lily.

'Not quite straight away.' Samuel frowned and Lily wasn't sure what she'd done wrong. 'You've a smudge of dust on your cheek.' He rubbed at it lightly with his thumb and then moved his fingers to tilt her face towards his. His lips met hers and Lily forgot all about the silver, Mabel and everything else except her beloved Samuel.

When they finally knocked on Mabel's bedroom door, they could hardly hear her reply. As the news was important, they decided to go in. It was immediately apparent that Mabel was very ill. She was in bed, the twins awake, but quiet in their cot beside her. Her skin was grey and her eyes, although open, looked unfocussed. Although she was shivering, perspiration was flowing down her face.

Lily went to her. 'Mrs Potts, I am sending Samuel for the doctor.'

Mabel struggled to sit up, but it was obvious she was exhausted. 'There is no money to spare for him.'

Lily and Samuel then sat beside Mabel and told her what they'd found in the attic. She seemed to rally a bit as she said, 'They were Mother and Father's. I wonder why Eta and I forgot about them? Things would have been much less of a worry for Eta.'

She started to pluck at the bedsheets, getting agitated again. She turned her head to look at Archie and Sylvan.

'Please, Lily, please, promise me you'll look after the children. They love you and I trust you with their well-being. Sell the silver and you will have money to live on. You can stay on here at the house when I'm dead if you promise you'll look after the children.'

'But what about Cecil?' asked Samuel. Lily was cross with him for bringing Cecil into the conversation to cause Mabel even more worry.

Mabel's voice was unexpectedly strong as she said, 'You don't need to worry about that, you'll never see him again.'

# 13

Lily had a lot to think about. The doctor had confirmed their fears that Mabel was weakening. The bad fortune at The Limes was never ending. And now she had to decide whether or not she, who had only wanted to be the maid, could take on the care of two children who weren't hers. She busied herself making chicken broth, hoping Mabel would eat some.

Samuel walked into the kitchen and sat at the table. 'I've just been in the shop and Bertha has said she'll do more hours to help out. Her family will be pleased to have some extra money.'

'That's one less thing to worry about, for now at least. There, the broth is simmering nicely. I do hope the doctor is wrong, but Mabel looks at death's door.'

Samuel beckoned her over and pulled out the chair next to his. 'Come and sit awhile. You have to think about what

Mabel has asked of you and maybe talking to someone will help.'

'Talking to you helps, Samuel. What am I to do? I can't abandon the children and yet I am not sure I am ready to, or even want to, be a mother to them. It isn't how I saw my life.'

'How did you see it?'

Lily didn't want to answer. She'd lain awake at night thinking of a life with Samuel. The two of them living in a tiny cottage. Samuel painting and writing, and her working at her sewing.

'I saw it differently.' 'Taking on the care of two children is a big responsibility.' Lily felt sad that he said nothing about him being in her future and sharing the care. He seemed fond of the children, but Lily wondered if he would stay on at The Limes or find somewhere else to live.

He continued, 'Then there's the question of money which could be worrying although the silver should be enough to live on, for a while anyway. We must get it valued. I will take it into town soon.'

Lily stood up.

'I have no choice. I can't abandon the babies. They are less than a year old. They know me and I love them. I will care for them like their mother. Now I will take the broth to Mabel and tell her my decision. Maybe by putting her mind at rest she will be less anxious and recover.'

Samuel stood up and brie.y held her hand. 'I will come with you.'

To Lily's disappointment, Mabel refused the broth. 'It might strengthen you, Mrs Potts, I made it especially for you.'

Mabel smiled weakly. 'You are very kind, dear Lily, but I have no appetite.' She was wracked by a fit of coughing.

Lily passed her some water. 'May I sit with you, please? I have made my decision.'

Mabel nodded her head.

Lily continued, 'I have given much thought to your question and have decided I will take on the care of the children should anything happen to you. I love them dearly.'

Mabel breathed out slowly.

'Oh, thank you! You will be a better mother to them than I could ever be. And you may live wherever you like. You can sell the house. It would be better to move from here, I think. A third of the house and everything else will be yours. I must re-write my will. Please ask Reverend Mason to come to the house.' She turned to Samuel. 'I am sure that between us, Samuel, we can write my new will, and you and the vicar can witness my signing of it. Please fetch him now, Lily. I must get it written.'

Mabel seemed calmer after the vicar's visit and the will was in place. Lily and Samuel sat with her, holding the babies on their laps so that she could see them. Then she closed her eyes and appeared to sleep.

'I am sure Mabel thinks Cecil is dead. If she is wrong and he is alive, shouldn't we find him and tell him his wife is dying?' Lily asked.

'What! After the way he behaved towards you and Mabel? He will never set foot in this house again if I have any say in it!'

'But he's her husband in the eyes of the law and God. He has the right to know.'

'He has no rights whatsoever. And where would you find him? You really want him in this house? And how is he going to feel about the will?' Samuel put Sylvan in the cot and paced the floor. 'Please, Lily, tell me you aren't going looking for him.'

'No, I thought you could.'

'I can't believe you! After what he attempted with you?'

'You would be here to protect me. It would just be until Mabel dies, although I can't bear to think about that.'

'No, Lily, we can't find him. He will just cause more trouble, you know it. You are too good and want to do what's best for people, but it would not be best thing for Mabel, the babies — or you.'

Lily knew he was being sensible. 'You are right again. It was another ridiculous idea.'

Mabel stirred and woke.

'You're all still here with me. I am glad,' she murmured. Reaching out she grasped Lily's hand. 'I have to tell you something. I have to confess. Oh, I truly cannot bear it!' Her face was etched with pain.

Lily didn't know how to help, but soon Mabel stopped moaning and was calm again.

'I hit him over the head,' Mabel whispered.

Samuel moved over to Lily and put his hand on her shoulder.

'I killed Cecil.' Mabel groaned again. 'It is agony. I long for death, for this pain to be gone. I hit him with the coal shovel. He was a brute to us and deceived poor people, taking their much needed money. I loathed him when I saw what he was truly like. And he humiliated me.' She sighed and closed her eyes again. Her rasping breaths were accompanied with whimpering.

Lily looked at Samuel who shrugged. Moments later Mabel gave another deep sigh and Lily knew she was dead.

Tears coursed down her cheeks. 'Poor Mabel!'

They both gazed at the woman they had loved.

Lily wiped her eyes. 'I told you, Samuel. I said she killed him.'

'It was the illness which affected her mind. Maybe she wanted to kill him, but she was frail. There is no way she could have hit him and disposed of his body.'

'It's very strange though. Think about it, Samuel.'

'I won't. I want to remember Mabel as the sweet, kind woman she was, not as a murderer.'

'Think of the clues. Remember the blood on the other side of the room and the mud on the hem of her skirt when she hadn't been out at all that day. Why didn't she reply when we knocked on her door to tell her Cecil had left? Where was she?

'And then there is the suitcase and the bicycle, both left behind. Surely he would have taken them with him. The day after his disappearance Mabel was exhausted and it is since then she has got worse and worse. What will it take to convince you? There are enough clues to show she killed him.'

'It does sound convincing, but I still doubt she would have the strength and stamina to kill him, let alone to dispose of him, as well as pack his things and move the bicycle.

'There must be simple explanations for your clues. Her fatigue, for example, is easily explained by the fact that Cecil had attacked her maid and had left the house. It was too much for Mabel to deal with.

'As for her confession, I believe her illness caused her to ramble. If she did kill him, where is his body?'

'We must tell the police,' said Lily.

'We'll do no such thing.'

'You may not, but I must.'

'They will tell you the same as me, that it is nonsense. And, if you insist, at least please wait until after her funeral. Let us give her a decent, peaceful burial.'

Samuel was gently insistent and Lily felt they were separated by their disagreement.

'Very well, but I will go to the police after that.'

'They will tell you it is nonsense,' he repeated. 'And you must think of Sylvan and Archie. Do you really want them to be thought of as the children of a murderer?'

# 14

Since their disagreement, Lily and Samuel had lost much of the warmth between them, but worked together when necessary. They had decided to sort through Mabel's possessions to see what should be kept and what got rid of. Lily pulled a drawer out of the dressing table, felt underneath it and at the back, and then replaced it before pulling out another.

'What are you doing? Is that really necessary? What do you expect to find?' Samuel asked.

'We don't want to miss anything. Just think, if we hadn't searched the attic thoroughly we would never have found the silver. I don't expect to find anything valuable, but you never know. You'd be surprised where people hide things.'

They made piles of clothes on the bed then Lily pulled out the drawer at the bottom of the wardrobe. She leaned in and felt around with her hand.

'Aha, you see,' she said pulling out a crumpled paper. After smoothing it out she handed it to Samuel. 'What does it say? I don't suppose I'll know all the words.'

Samuel began to read . . .

'I am writing this confession the night of my husband's death. I need to unburden myself, but I will not tell anyone because I do not want to be separated from my children. It happened after I had heard a commotion in the kitchen. When I went to investigate, Cecil had a bad head wound. He struggled to get up, staggered towards me and mauled me. I was incensed when he sneered at me and said he only married me because he couldn't dominate Eta. The wound made him weaker than he would otherwise have been.

'Cecil had behaved despicably throughout our marriage and I seized the opportunity I had been waiting for to rid myself of him once and for all. I hit him over the head with the coal shovel. I finished him off. I found a strength I have

194

never felt before.

'I know I have done a wicked thing by killing him, but that is what I did and I shall suffer for it for as long as I live.'

Lily let out a long, weary breath. 'Her deathbed confession was true,' she said, quietly.

'You were right all along. Shall I continue?'

Lily nodded.

'After I had hit him he seemed to find an extraordinary power to drag himself out of the house. I watched him as blood poured from the wound on his head. After recovering from the shock, I tried to follow him to see where he would go as he seemed in a very bad way. There was no sign of him.

'I don't know what happened to him as there is no possibility he could have survived. I've spent days and nights worrying that his body would be found and I would be charged with his murder, but now I believe he must have struggled along the lane and then died and fallen into the river.

'I went back upstairs where I packed his things in his suitcase and put them in the shed. Then I threw his bicycle in the hedge so it would look as though he had left of his own accord.

'Now I am glad the world is rid of him, but I am sorry for my children. Not because their father is dead, but because their mother is a murderer.

Once I was back in my room I felt drained, sick and weak, but I wanted to write this in order for the truth to be known in the future. I shall be eternally damned.'

Neither of them spoke for a while then Samuel said, 'It is a terrible thing to say, but it was probably good she killed him. He might have gone on to do even more desperate things.'

'What do you mean?'

'About ten years ago, when I was young and impressionable, so it affected me, there was a story in the news which everyone talked about of two sisters who murdered people to claim the life insurance money.'

'Cecil wouldn't have resorted to that, would he?' Lily gasped.

'We are saved from finding out. And we know very little about his past. What had he done before he arrived here looking for a new start?'

Lily shivered.

'The women, Margaret Higgins and Catherine Flanagan, were found guilty and hanged.'

'How terrible. I can't imagine such an awful thing happening.'

'The first suspicions were aroused when the husband of Margaret Higgins died in his thirties after less than a year of marriage. His brother had doubts about Thomas's death and alerted the authorities. When it was discovered he had been killed by arsenic, the bodies of three other people, who had died in the home the sisters shared, including Catherine's son, were exhumed. They had all died from arsenic poisoning and each also had insurance policies taken out on their lives.

'It seemed that the women chose a

lodger or relative to insure, often without the person's knowledge, and would pay the premiums themselves if necessary. Once the victim was dead, money was paid out by the insurance company.'

Lily couldn't believe there were such scheming people who would kill their own family for money. But Cecil could well have murdered Mabel, and maybe the rest of the household too, if he'd stood to gain financially. She felt sick when she thought of Sylvan and Archie.

Samuel continued. 'It's simple enough. Cecil wouldn't have had a problem. We sold fly papers in the shop. You simply soak them in water to obtain the arsenic. The sisters administered the solution to their victims over several days until they died.'

Lily sat silently.

'I am sorry, Lily, I shouldn't have told you, but I think we should be grateful to Mabel for removing Cecil from the world. And I am sorry I didn't believe you. You were clever to see the signs. I will take more notice of you in future.'

In spite of the circumstances and the shocking story he had just told her, Lily was pleased he was talking about a future which included her.

Work at The Limes should have been easier for Lily with just Archie and Sylvan to look after. She still felt obliged to go through the usual cleaning routine she'd carried out since her arrival. Mabel's funeral had been a dismal affair for Samuel and her. They'd sat close together in a front pew at the church and Lily had tugged at the fabric of her black mourning dress. She was sure Mabel wouldn't have minded her taking the dress she'd worn to her sister's funeral and altering it to fit her. Buying a new one would have been another expense. Samuel still hadn't taken the silver from the attic to be valued and sold, so money was scarce and they'd wanted to buy a coffin which would make Mabel proud.

Bertha had been willing to look after the twins during the service. Neither Lily nor Samuel wanted Archie and Sylvan to be present at the church. Lily was ashamed to feel a shred of release when they'd returned to the house. And now, two weeks later, life was going on much as it had before, albeit without Mabel.

'Lily, you look exhausted,' said Samuel, coming into the parlour after returning from town. 'Can't you put the children to bed?'

Lily laughed. 'Poor little things. They're sleeping better at night now and so need some more time to play during the day.' She yawned and rubbed her eyes. 'I am tired. And so must you be. You've been going in to serve in the shop, painting your pictures, looking after the children and still finding time to teach me to read and write.'

'I've been thinking about things.' Samuel sat on a chair and offered a toy soldier to Archie, who made a grab for it, holding on to Samuel's leg as he did so. Lily found the scene delightful. Samuel would be a loving father. She had no time to dwell on that idea as he was continuing, 'We could close the shop. It would mean there would be no income from it and Bertha would not have a job, but we would have more time to manage the house and children and the things we want to do rather than what we feel we should do. What do you think?'

'I don't go into the shop much, so it would mean you would have the time.' 'Yes, I suppose it sounds selfish, doesn't it?

I meant that I could spend the time helping you around the house, looking after the children, that sort of thing.'

Lily thought it sounded an excellent idea and would be more than happy for Samuel to spend more time with her.

'What about the money, though? Of course, I shall still have to send money home to my mother. Will there be enough to feed and clothe the children? I promised Mabel I would care for them and I'd like to do it properly. How did it go in town this morning?'

Samuel grinned. 'I have sold the silver, as you said I should, for a considerable amount of money. If you agree I will ask the bank if they can look after it for you and release a certain amount each month.'

'Is that secure? I keep thinking of Cecil and how dishonest he was. Do you think the bank is safe?' Lily gnawed at her fingernail.

'Yes, I do, but I can ask Reverend Mason's opinion, if you like.'

Lily felt uncomfortable. 'It sounds as if I don't trust you, Samuel.' She moved closer to him. 'I do, you know. I'd trust you with my life.'

Samuel's mouth was almost on hers when Sylvan, who was on the floor, banged her on the leg with a doll and giggled.

'Little monkey,' laughed Lily, scooping her up and hugging her. The small child put her face close to Lily's and it was as if she were kissing her. It was a beautiful gesture and Lily was full of love for her, but it would have been so much nicer if she'd had the chance to kiss Samuel too.

'There will always be another time,' he said, dropping a swift kiss on her forehead. 'I'll go into the shop and later we can decide if we're agreedabout closing it. Then we'll have to break the news to Bertha.'

When the time came to tell Bertha about closing the shop, she came to them first with her news. 'I know it will be letting you down,' she said, 'but I don't think I can work in the shop any longer. My daughter is expecting, you see, and what with her moving house, my Walter and I have decided to go with her.'

'Bertha, what exciting news,' said Lily, hugging her. 'We'll miss you, of course we will, and so will Archie and Sylvan. But we were thinking of shutting the shop anyway, so don't feel you are putting us out.'

'We were wondering how to break the news to you actually, Bertha,' said Samuel.

At the end of the week, Lily, Samuel, Bertha and the twins had a tea party. Lily had baked a cherry cake and some ginger buns, using Mabel's recipes and ingredients from the shop. There were also roast beef sandwiches and some minced meat pies.

'You're a good cook, Lily,' said Bertha. 'I expect Samuel considers himself very lucky to be on the receiving end of your food.'

'I do indeed, Bertha,' said Samuel, smiling at Lily who was helping the twins drink their milk.

With the shop shut, it was easy to work out a new routine. The cleaning had to be done, of course, but Samuel was faithful to his word and helped her, keeping an eye on the twins while she cleaned and cooked. Then, she took over looking after the children while he went out painting.

There was time now for reading and writing lessons and Lily felt proud to send her mother letters she had written herself.

Sometimes a reply from home came back, dictated to the vicar by her mother, and her confidence soared as she read it out to Samuel, who prompted her with the words she couldn't read, which were becoming fewer as she improved.

After one such lesson, Samuel said, 'You're doing well, Lily, but I'd like to spend my time with you in a different way. Let's all enjoy each other's company, shall we?'

They went out into the garden and sat under the lime trees. There were two, one of which was stronger than the other. It was in a better position in the garden and more sheltered. Samuel put the children on the grass and Lily picked a few leaves from a low branch. She knelt down and tickled first Sylvan then Archie with them, making them laugh. Then she noticed something she hadn't seen before. 'Look, Samuel, the leaves are heart-shaped.'

'Yes, this is our tree, the love tree.'

He sat beside her and took the leaf she was holding out to him. Then he pulled her to him, cradling her in his arms. When his lips met hers, Lily experienced the joy she had felt at every other embrace with Samuel.

She was the first to break away, remembering her duty to Archie and Sylvan; she shouldn't neglect them. They were still playing happily beneath the lime tree. She glanced up at its top and wondered if it really were her and Samuel's tree of love. What a romantic thought.

'Is it really our tree of love?' she whispered to Samuel.

He nodded and drew Lily near to him again.

She was content to lie in his arms daydreaming happily about the two of them.

Then her mind went back to Mabel and how unhappy she had been when she died. If only Mabel could have found love with a man as loveable as Samuel, instead of a brute like Cecil. She shivered as she thought of Cecil.

Sitting bolt upright, she remembered she must go to the police and tell them of Mabel's confession. Samuel had said to leave it until after the funeral and now that was over. If she reminded Samuel it would break the romantic spell, but she felt she must tell him now. Surely he would understand her motive of wanting to be honest.

After she'd told him she was going to the police, he said, 'Lily, I told you it was not a good idea. No one will believe you. Let things carry on as they are,' he said. 'Who knows what would happen if you stir things up?'

They settled into their new routine and Lily enjoyed her time with the children although she was constantly exhausted. She looked forward to the evenings when she and Samuel had time to themselves. He occasionally cooked their evening meal and one day he delighted her with a dish called Rabbit Surprised, having caught the rabbit himself. The succulent rabbit with the added flavours of parsley, lemon peel, butter, cream and boiled egg yolk was delicious.

He would come in from short outings foraging, excited with what he had found. 'Look what I have brought you today. Beech nuts. We can eat them raw or cook them.'

He also brought her posies of flowers from the garden or wild flowers from the fields and hedgerows.

What she found most romantic of all was when he wrote a poem for her and now she could usually read his poems herself. His handwriting was elegant, and she kept everything he wrote and gave her, tied together with a ribbon.

She'd learnt her favourite poem by rote and often recited it to herself: You are my sun, Who warms me, You are my star, Who guides me. You are my moon, Who lights my darkness. You are my Lily, I love thee.

As she tidied the kitchen, Samuel busied himself writing on a sheet of paper. 'There, I've finished. I've written a song for the girl I love.'

'Who might that be?' she asked, grinning.

'It might be a girl in the village or it might be you.' He grabbed at her waist as she passed and pulled her onto his lap, covering her face in kisses. 'You know I love you, Lily Harrison, and would do anything for you.'

'I love you too, Samuel. Now sing me your song.'

'It's your song.' He sang the song in his strong, honeyed voice and when he had finished Lily clapped gleefully.

'It's beautiful. I never thought a man would write a song and sing it to me. A love song too. Thank you, Samuel.'

'I would like to be with just you more often, but you are always too busy with Archie and Sylvan to think about me.' He was sullen.

Lily pulled away from him. 'Really Samuel, that is very sel.sh.'

'I understand why you have to spend so much time looking after the children, but I am jealous.'

'I don't know how you think I could choose between Archie and Sylvan, and you. I have taken on the duty of looking after the children and must keep my promise to Mabel and do it.'

'And I love you for that. You are a kind, caring, honest, truly good person and I admire you. I am not good enough for you, being thoughtless and selfish. I'm sorry.'

Lily was sad. Samuel loved her, but

it seemed that taking on the care of the babies may have spoiled their relationship. She couldn't give him the attention he clearly longed for and it was possible he would be lost to her.

# 15

A fog had descended on not just the house, but on Lily as well. When she heard Samuel coming through the front door, she wiped her tears and remained seated at the table as he walked into the kitchen.

'It's a typical November day, Lily,' he said, rubbing his hands together and blowing into them. 'Cold, damp and miserable. You look miserable too. What's wrong? Usually you are preparing our mid-day meal at this time.' He moved over to her and put his hands on her shoulders.

'You will have to leave us,' she managed to gasp. 'I will be all right for money even though you won't be contributing anything to the household. As you know, one of my brothers has left home to work, so my mother doesn't need as much money from me.'

'I don't understand. Why are you saying such a thing? Are you unwell? Why would I leave? We are getting along fine. Better than that. I adore you.'

She stood and threw herself into his arms. 'And I adore you. I wondered why some of the villagers were turning their backs on me. Now I know.'

'What is it?' Samuel gently moved a strand of hair from her face and pushed it behind her ear.

'I went for a walk with the babies tucked up warmly in their pram. I overheard some of the village women talking among themselves. They think it is not right, they said sinful, for a single woman and man to be living in the same house.'

'These are the same women who cheerfully acknowledge us to our faces! Women who shopped here and talked to us in a friendly manner. We won't take any notice of them. What business is it of theirs? We are happy and we are providing a secure home for the children. Orphaned children. How can that be sinful?' asked Samuel.

'It is the children we must think of. They said it isn't a good situation in which to bring up the children.'

'But the children's mother was a murderer! They accepted Mabel and thought she was a good mother.' Samuel roughly ran his hands through his hair.

'They don't know what she did and she was a wonderful mother,' Lily said.

'If they knew she'd killed her husband, they would surely allow us to get on with our innocent lives and do our best for Archie and Sylvan.'

'All they see is how we live.' Lily sighed.

'You want me to go, and leave everything for you to do? You are exhausted anyway and I help, don't I? With the children, even household tasks, in the garden, cutting wood, lighting fires.'

'You do and I am grateful. It has been good to share everything with you, but I have come to a decision. We must put our feelings aside and you must move out of the house for the sake of the children and me.'

The pain on his face was unbearable to see. She gently pushed him to one side and left the room at once.

Lily longed to escape to her room and give vent to her feelings. Sylvan and Archie wailed at the same time and she knew she must see to them. Hadn't she just given up the man she loved for their sake? She told herself to avoid feeling resentful towards them. Sylvan was hungry and Archie became slow and dreamy when he heard her voice. She hugged them both to her and took them to the kitchen. Relief flooded through her to find Samuel had gone elsewhere.

Lily threw an old blanket on the floor and sat Archie on it with a few toys. As she fed Sylvan, thoughts about her ability as an adoptive mother surfaced. Was she looking after the children properly and how would she manage when Samuel had gone? If only her own mother was close enough to help and advise her. How young and vulnerable she felt and escaping by running away for a few days appealed. Calming down, she told herself she would manage on her own and be as independent as possible. Thoughts of Eta tumbled into her head. For Eta, self-reliance had surfaced along with her disappointment at being a spinster and childless.

With Sylvan fed and happy again she put her on the blanket with her brother. Lily began to sing, but stopped abruptly when Samuel walked into the room with two pieces of luggage.

He stood at the other side of the room and put the bags down, a frown on his face. 'I do not care what people think of me, but I do care about your reputation and those two little ones.' He nodded towards the children. 'I am leaving now and, if it is all right with you, I will call for my other belongings when I have found permanent rooms.'

He walked towards her and wrapped his arms around her. Their lips met and Lily realised it could be the last kiss she received from her darling man. When they pulled apart he bent and gave both children a kiss on the cheek before hurrying from the room.

Lily tried to keep her emotions in check, but on hearing the front door close she burst into tears. Archie and Sylvan both looked at her and their bottom lips trembled.

'It's all right. We will be all right.'

In spite of her words, she felt sad and lonely. The loneliest she'd felt since arriving at The Limes. It would be hard being without Samuel after the love and companionship they'd shared, but she and the children would be strong together.

How would Samuel find being on his own after having a family to love and cherish? What if he found someone else to love? It was a hard prospect to consider and one which broke her heart.

# 16

Lily enjoyed looking after Archie and Sylvan and was able to keep her spirits up when she switched her thoughts from Samuel. The household tasks still had to be carried out, but she changed her routine a little to get used to being in the parlour and the dining room as, before Mabel's death, she'd spent most of her time in the house either upstairs or in the kitchen.

Somehow the kitchen reminded her of time spent with Samuel and, apart from preparing meals, she stayed out of there as much as she could. Each day she tried to take the children out in the fresh air, although it was now sometimes cold and wet.

As she wheeled them away from the house, her thoughts turned to the love tree and Samuel, and her heart lurched.

The first few times she'd ventured into the village, she was torn between wishing for adult company and having to run the gauntlet of the village women gossiping about her and had tried to avoid them. One day, however, she held her head high and marched towards a group of them.

'Good morning, Lily,' said Mrs Cousins, who had been a frequent customer in the shop. 'Those twins are looking happy.' She peered into the pram.

'Yes, they're beautiful children. I love looking after them,' replied Lily.

Ada Markham sniffed, making Lily feel a little nervous. 'I think you did the right thing, Lily. Samuel and you should not have been under the same roof. It was moral of you to kick him out.'

Lily bristled. 'We agreed to do what was best for the children. He's a very decent man.'

All Ada did was nod her head, but the fact she'd backed down pleased Lily.

'We miss our visits to the shop at The Limes, and also Eta and Mabel,' said Cora Archer. 'I don't know what happened to Cecil Potts, but I was pleased when he wasn't around any longer.' The

218

rest of the women were in agreement. 'I was just saying to the others that I would like them to come to my house tomorrow and have a cup of tea with me. Would you like to come, Lily? And the children, of course.'

'I shall look forward to that,' said Lily.

The visit to Cora's house had been enjoyable and Lily decided to invite the group to The Limes one afternoon, even though it meant spending time in the kitchen baking cakes.

She thought back to the occasion of Mabel's birthday party and the party they'd had when Bertha left the shop. They'd been happy times and Lily was excited to be welcoming the group of women from the village who she hoped would be her friends. For a moment, she considered it strange that the people who had been responsible for parting her from Samuel were now becoming her closest companions. Then she shook the idea from her mind and started planning the tea-party.

While the snow cake and currant buns

were cooling, Lily picked some greenery, and a few asters which were still in
bloom, from the garden, put the twins in
their pram and walked to the graveyard.
She visited the graves of Eta, Mabel and
their parents on a regular basis, wanting
Archie and Sylvan to grow up knowing
about their family.

When she returned, she dressed the
children in clean clothes. Then she
wondered what she should wear. Since
being at the house, Lily had been used
to wearing her uniform, but now she
was no longer a maid. Hoping neither
Eta nor Mabel would mind, she looked
through the wardrobe in her bedroom
and selected a dress which had probably
been their mother's. It was a dark purple silk and fitted her well. The reflection
from the cheval mirror pleased her.

The table was already laid in the parlour when Ada arrived. 'Oh, this does
look lovely,' she exclaimed.

'Please sit down,' invited Lily. 'The
children can play on the floor.'

A few minutes later everyone else was

there and they made themselves at home.

'I've never been in here,' said Mrs Cousins. 'The shop was just through that door, wasn't it?' she asked, pointing.

The chatting continued and Lily went to make the tea. When she returned to the parlour, Archie and Sylvan were the centre of attention.

'We were saying what a very good mother you are, Lily,' said Cora, cuddling Sylvan. 'These two are beautifully cared for, it's obvious.'

The others joined in with words of praise for Lily's mothering and home-making skills which made her feel good about herself.

She enjoyed the afternoon and was quite sorry when the women stood and said their farewells.

The house was quiet without them and the twins were tired from all the attention they'd been given. She smiled as she looked at their cake-smeared faces and went to get a cloth to clean them up. Then she cleared the parlour and washed the dishes. It would have been nice to have shared the remains of the cake with Samuel, she thought, her throat constricting with tears she refused to shed.

Later, she slipped into the garden and stood under the lime tree Samuel had said was their love tree. She was constantly drawn to it, hoping to bring him closer to her, but a tree was no substitute for the man she adored.

In the sanctuary of her bedroom that night, Lily took out Samuel's poems and she put her finger to the paper and slowly read them aloud, wanting to refresh her memory of his words, but also to maintain her reading skills.

Little did she know she could have done with them the following morning, when an official looking letter arrived. It was addressed to her, but she didn't open it.

When the twins were washed, fed and dressed, she squeezed them once again into the pram. They were getting too big to both fit into it and she wondered if the expense of a pushchair could be justified, especially as they'd be walking soon.

With the letter tucked beside them, she wheeled the pram to the vicar, who she knew would help her read the letter.

'Come in, Lily,' said Reverend Mason, beaming at her. 'And it's good to see Archie and Sylvan again. They're looking well. You must be doing an excellent job as their mother.'

Lily could feel her cheeks heating at his compliment. 'I've got a letter and I wonder if you can help me as I can't read very well.'

'Of course. Let's look at it together, shall we?'

After a good few minutes, Harold said, 'The letter is from The East Anglian Insurance Company and they say they've had other complaints about Cecil Potts. And they thank you for getting in touch and alerting them to his dishonest ways.'

Lily was surprised they'd taken the trouble to thank her, but it made her feel useful to know she'd been helpful to them.

'They also say,' continued Harold, 'that they assume Mr Potts was looking for respectability by marrying Mabel Stratford and was probably escaping from his dubious past when he had set up similar swindles in other parts of the country. They ask where Cecil is now as they'd like to ask him some questions.'

'We should reply to them,' said Lily, wondering how she was going to get herself out of this mess. Cecil was dead, murdered, but she couldn't tell the insurance company that and she couldn't lie to the vicar. She hesitated before saying, 'He won't be returning.'

'I see,' said Harold. 'I'm not surprised, I must say. He wouldn't get a very warm welcome from the people around here.'

'I should let the insurance company know, shouldn't I?'

'Would you like me to write the letter with you?' asked the vicar.

'Oh, would you? Yes, please. I can form some words, but nothing like a business letter.'

The two of them moved to the desk and Harold took a fresh sheet of paper and had his pen poised. 'You tell me what you'd like to put and I'll write it. Then we'll read it together to make sure it's what you want to send. Is that acceptable?'

Lily was not happy when she left Harold Mason and hoped the letter he'd written on her behalf was right for the insurance company. If only she could discuss things with Samuel. That was a vain hope as she had no idea where he was staying. Perhaps he would send her a letter, but if he did, would she be able to read it? She decided that when she got back to The Limes she would carry on with the reading exercises Samuel had given her.

Samuel occupied her thoughts as she traipsed home with the children, passing familiar landmarks. It was almost two years since she'd arrived at The Limes and met Samuel and the Stratford sisters. She had hoped to talk to Samuel when he'd collected the rest of his possessions, but he'd sent a man with a handcart to collect them. Never seeing Samuel again was a thought she couldn't bear.

As Christmas drew closer, Lily tried to stay cheerful for the sake of the children. Remembering the previous festive season when Cecil had put a dampener on their spirits, she was determined to make sure Archie and Sylvan had a happy time and knew how loved they were.

One evening when she was busy in the parlour wrapping some small gifts for the children, the vicar and her few village friends, there was a knock at the front door. It was dark, the wind was howling and rain was lashing at the windows.

The first person who came to mind was Cecil. Her heart pounded. It couldn't be him. Mabel had been sure she had killed him. The thought made her shiver.

After Christmas the authorities would be told the truth. It was impossible to live with the dishonesty of keeping his murder quiet.

The knocking started again. Maybe someone was in trouble. She stood in the hall and called, 'Who is it?'

There was a muffled reply. Then in a lull in the storm she recognised Samuel's voice. 'Lily, please let me in. I'm drenched.'

She opened the door and Samuel rushed in, slamming it shut behind him.

Lily was shocked to see him.

'This is a surprise. What a mess you look. Let me help you take your hat and coat off.' She hung the dripping garments on the coatstand and led him to the kitchen. 'I'll get something to warm you up and then you can explain why you are here. There is some leftover soup.'

She busied herself heating the soup and cutting chunks of bread. After placing the food in front of him she sat at the table, confused by his arrival at the house.

'How are you, Samuel?'

'Better now I've seen you. It's been a nightmare, not seeing or hearing you, not touching you. I have had time to think about you, about us. I had to see you.'

'I have thought of you every day too. It has been lonely and difficult without you,' Lily confessed.

'I'm sorry if you have been unhappy,

but we decided together it was for the best. How are the children?'

'Sweet and funny. They cheer me up when I am missing you. But why are you here? I don't imagine you were just passing in this weather.'

Lily almost wished he hadn't come as he would have to go again. Seeing him brought back strong emotions, she wanted to reach out to touch him.

'I can't stand not being with you and the children. You three are my family. My love for you brought me back and I would like to live here with you again.'

How easy it would be to say yes, and how difficult to live with the consequences.

Trying to sound strong, she said, 'You know that's impossible. We can't live in the same house. It was all right when Eta and Mabel were alive, but just the two of us with the children would be too difficult. Eat your soup and then you must go.'

Samuel crumbled the bread as they sat in silence. 'I can't live without you,

Lily. I am besotted with you and devoted to you. I am a broken man. You make me whole. We have to be together, you know it as well as I do.'

'We shouldn't have to suffer like this. There is nothing I can do about the situation.'

'There is something you can do. You can say yes.' Samuel leapt up and his chair clattered to the floor. He rushed round to Lily's side of the table, knelt in front of her and took her hand. 'Lily Harrison, will you marry me?'

Lily couldn't believe what he was saying.

'You want me to be your wife?'

'I do. Say yes, I beg you.'

'Yes, yes, oh yes!'

Samuel smothered her face in kisses. Lily felt whole now that she was close to her precious love, and she gave herself up to his embrace.

# 17

'Ding dong! merrily on high in heav'n the bells are ringing. Ding dong! verily the sky is riv'n with angel singing. Gloria, Hosanna in excelsis!'

Lily was feeling festive and enjoying singing carols as they hung Christmas decorations in the parlour. She had been busy for several evenings making paper cornucopias and decorating them with pictures and ribbons. Filled with sweets and with a cotton threaded through the top of each one they were ready to hang alongside the gilded and silver walnuts already on the tree.

Samuel stood back and admired their efforts.

'The tree is looking impressive and the holly and ivy along the mantelpiece looks grand.'

'I like the mistletoe ball we made yesterday best.' Lily giggled.

'Come here then.'

She walked over to stand under it with him and they kissed.

He held her away from him and looked in her eyes. 'This is going to be a very special Christmas for us. We can forget the past difficulties and the awful time we had last year.'

However, that was the problem. Lily could not forget Cecil.

'Why are you frowning?'

'If I tell you, please don't be annoyed. The trouble is I can't fully enjoy the festivities because there is unfinished business concerning Cecil.'

'I see.' Samuel turned away from her.

'The thought of Cecil's body not having been found worries me. I think he should have a Christian burial in spite of his wickedness. Now I've spoilt this evening. I'm sorry, Samuel, but I can't forget him.'

'Then we must do something about it. I can't have my future wife . . . just think of that, Lily, we will be husband and wife soon . . . worrying about a dead body. We will tell the police. I disliked the man intensely and he caused misery to countless families as well as his own, but we will do as you want. Although how the police will know where Cecil is, I've no idea. Come on, Lily, cheer up, at least a bit.'

'There is something else too. I miss my family and wish I could visit them.' Lily didn't want to sound as though she was moaning, but she needed to share her feelings with him.

'Then we will go together with the children.'

'No, it would be too much trouble for my mum as she has enough to do and too many mouths to feed already.'

'You always think of other people, never yourself. Cecil was wicked and yet you want a Christian burial for him if his body can be found. You'd like to visit your family and yet you think it will be too much for your mother. What a lovely woman you are! I am the luckiest man alive. Why don't you write your family a letter? You could tell them about our preparations for Christmas. I am impressed you have continued with reading and writing while I have been away. Now I am staying with Cora things are easier. It's good of her to have taken me in at such short notice.'

'Will she be a good landlady?'

'She's a lovely person. With me spending my days and having all my meals here we won't see much of each other, but I think the arrangement could work well.'

'I don't like it when you leave.'

'Soon we will be married and then I will never leave you again.'

That was exactly what Lily wanted. To be with Samuel for ever. But there were also the twins to consider. She knew he loved them almost as much, if not the same, as she did. Although she'd raised the subject of Cecil's murder to Samuel, she felt there was more to discuss. 'You're looking forward to an already completed family?' she asked.

'Archie and Sylvan as well as you, do you mean? I don't view the four of us as a necessarily completed family.' Samuel smiled broadly.

Lily's insides trembled. Did he mean he would like them to have a baby of their own? It was something she'd given much thought to.

'I can think of nothing better than the four of us at the moment, although I don't want them to be have the reputation of having a murdering mother and a swindler for a father,' said Samuel.

'They will have to know the truth when they're older, but by then they will be secure enough with our love to be able to get through the situation.'

Samuel rubbed his chin. 'Maybe we should consider moving.'

'Moving from The Limes, do you mean? But it's the babies' home! They were born here and spent happy times with their real mother. We can't uproot them from their home, Samuel, can we?' Lily felt bewildered by the decisions she would have to take on behalf of the children.

'It's your home, too,' said Samuel, gently stroking her face.

'But I can live with any changes,'

croaked Lily. 'They're just children.'

'Sit down and I'll make tea,' said Samuel.

While he was out of the room, Lily nestled into a chair and gazed at the Christmas tree. It was looking very festive. The twins would love it. She thought back to their birth and then the day Mabel had asked her to take care of them. Even if Mabel hadn't made financial provision for the arrangement, Lily would have done her very best not to be separated from the babies. Suddenly she sat up straight and thought about what Mabel had said.

'Here you are,' said Samuel placing a cup and saucer on the table beside Lily.

'Samuel! We could sell the house and have a third share.'

'Yes, that's right, but a minute ago you didn't want to move the children from their home.'

'I know. And I'm still not sure. But maybe, just maybe, it would be better to start afresh away from the memories of this house. It would suit me not to be reminded of Cecil every time I look at the faint discolouration that's still on the kitchen floor. Poor Mabel said it would be a good idea to move and start afresh. I'm beginning to think she was right.'

'I'd like you to be able to rest easy, Lily,' said Samuel, sipping his tea.

'But is it right for the children?' insisted Lily.

'What you said about it being their home is true and always will be. They were born here there's no escaping that fact. However, if you — and it is you — sell the house, their share of the money from the sale of The Limes will be put into trust for when they grow up.'

'Yes, I see. So they'll still have something from the house. Are you telling me to sell?'

'Certainly not!' said Samuel, looking horrified. 'It's completely up to you.' He put down his cup and held her hand tightly. 'I couldn't care less where we live, just as long as we're together.'

Lily closed her eyes. 'We could rent a little cottage, like the one I can see in my head at the moment.'

But when she opened her eyes, Samuel was bending over her, his lips about to taste hers. This time, she reached her arms around his neck and pulled him to her.

'I want you to stay with me.'

'My love, I'll be with you every minute I can, apart from the time I must spend with Cora for the sake of you and the children.'

Lily woke early as usual the following morning. Without opening her eyes, she sat on the edge of the bed and listened for the children. There was no sound from them. Then her eyes snapped open and she flopped back on the bed.

It was Christmas Day.

She would not be cleaning the house, but there was cooking to be done and fun to be had. The Christmas present she had promised herself was to stay in bed which was a luxury she hadn't enjoyed for two years. Snuggling under the eiderdown cover, she thought of Samuel and wished he were here beside her. She knew it was not a very moral thought, but it was what she wanted. Her love for him was endless.

'I can't believe I'll be married soon,' she whispered to herself. What would her family think? Mother would be happy she was sure and her father and brothers would wish her well and want to meet the 'unlucky' man as they would joke. She must send a letter to them as soon as the festivities were over.

The familiar sound of Archie and Sylvan waking up brought her back to the present. Falling into the usual routine, she changed and dressed them, telling them excitedly that it was Christmas Day and Samuel would be with them soon. They giggled at her, and Sylvan put her arm around her brother and gave him a light pat on the face.

With the three of them in very good humour, Lily took the children to the parlour where they were mesmerised by the decorations and tree. They reached out for the sparkly ornaments and Sylvan was eager to grasp the snowflakes Lily had made. It had all been worth the effort of making the house look festive and Lily was very pleased to see the effect on the children. She couldn't wait for Samuel to join them.

In the meantime, Lily sang carols she'd sung with her family over the years. They seemed to like the sound of her voice, but she knew her singing was not always tuneful.

'Merry Christmas!' At last Samuel was at the house. Sylvan reached out for him, her face lighting up. He took her in his arms and twirled her around. Then he enveloped Archie in the cuddle.

'What about me?' teased Lily, joining the three of them. 'This is the happiest Christmas I've ever had.' Then she remembered the children hadn't eaten. She reached out to take Archie, but he clung onto Samuel and so did his sister. 'I'll go and prepare the breakfast,' she said, going towards the kitchen.

'I'll stay with the children,' said Samuel, setting them down on the floor, 'unless I can help. Please don't cook anything for me as Cora fattened me up with the biggest meal I've ever seen. I don't think I'll need to eat for another week.'

'Lucky you, being waited on,' Lily teased.

She laid the table in the dining room and carried through bread, porridge and tea. With the large Christmas meal they were having later in the day, that would be enough, she decided.

The four of them sat around the table and Samuel helped the children to eat and not smear their breakfast over the table and high chairs, while Lily was able to concentrate on her own breakfast without having to supervise them.

He poured her a second cup of tea and she sighed. 'It's nice being looked after,' she said.

'You'll have to get used to it,' said Samuel. 'When we're together all the time, I won't let you do anything except lie around and take life easy.'

Archie let out a squeal and Sylvan hit

him with her spoon. Soon the two of them were crying and the morning peace was destroyed. Quickly, Samuel scooped up Sylvan and left the room. Lily helped Archie finish his bread soaked in milk, gave him a cuddle and then took him to the parlour where she found the other two.

'Present time, I think,' she said, placing Archie on the floor alongside Sylvan.

The two of them appeared best of friends now, for which Lily was grateful. She took two packages from under the tree and gave one each to the children. Archie tried to put his in his mouth, but Sylvan tore at the paper and crowed with delight when she saw a peg doll which Lily had made. She started playing with it until she saw Archie struggling with his present. Flinging her doll on the floor, she shuffled towards her brother and tore at the wrapping paper, revealing a stuffed cow made from spotted brown material Lily had found in a drawer in her room.

'Your turn now,' said Samuel, passing

her a large parcel. 'I smuggled it into my room on one of my visits. I hoped you wouldn't find it.'

'I don't go in there, not even to clean,' confessed Lily, easing the paper off. 'This is exciting, I didn't expect any presents this year. I wrote to Mum and said not to waste money on buying me anything. I hope she bought a large turkey with the money she saved.'

'Hurry up, Lily, you're the slowest person I know at opening presents. Don't you want to know what's in the parcel?'

Lily hurried with the last piece of wrapping and then exclaimed, 'Samuel, this is beautiful!' Tears brimmed her eyes as she looked at the painting he'd given her. 'Our lime tree,' she breathed.

'Our love tree,' said Samuel, softly.

He took the painting from her and laid it on a chair, then he put his arms around her. As his mouth lowered to hers, he said, 'I love you, Lily, I adore you.'

It was a magical moment for Lily to be kissed like that on Christmas Day and to be told by the person she loved most in the whole world that he loved her back.

The twins made their presence known as they reached for the Christmas tree and nearly pulled it over, and Samuel released his grip on Lily. He handed a brightly wrapped present to each of the children and bent down to help them rip off the paper. Archie appeared thrilled with his pull along duck and Sylvan was in raptures with her pull along pig.

'They're lovely,' said Lily. 'Where did you find them?'

'I made them,' said Samuel. 'The evenings were long without the three of you.' He looked sad for a moment and then laughed, 'You can see my artistic nature and imagination, can't you?'

'Samuel, I have a present for you.' Lily felt shy as she passed him a small flat parcel.

'Why, Lily, you didn't even know I would be home. You are very kind, thank you.'

Lily hugged his mention of home tightly inside her. 'Do you like it?'

Samuel unfolded the square of cotton.

It was a handkerchief on which she had embroidered his name.

'It's beautiful. And your handwriting and spelling are perfect! I shall carry it with me always. Thank you. It reminds me of the birthday present you gave Mabel.' He reached for her hand. 'I'm glad we're having a happier Christmas this year.'

'I don't want any reminders of Cecil and how wicked he was.' The reference to Cecil dampened the morning. Lily wondered if they'd ever be rid of the memory of Cecil Potts.

Before the Christmas meal was ready, Lily couldn't help but brighten up. The church service was uplifting and then the children and Samuel's antics had her laughing out loud. Some of her time was spent cooking the Christmas dinner and laying the table with the best crockery, cutlery and glasses although she resisted giving Sylvan and Archie any. When everything was ready they all sat in the dining room and Samuel produced a bag of oranges.

'Cora sent these,' he said as he handed

them to Lily.

'That's kind of her. I hope you have an appetite now in spite of your big breakfast at her house.'

'It all smells delicious. I'm sure we'll do it proud.' He felt in his pocket. 'Here we are, Lily, a kiss for you.'

She took the twist of coloured, fringed paper and unwrapped it. A sweet fell out and a piece of paper with some writing.

'Go on, read it.'

'My love is bigger than the sea, Lily, will you marry me?' She giggled. 'You know I will.'

'The verse is not my best, but I had to rush to write it after breakfast and I didn't want to be too late getting here.'

'I have not made a kiss for you.'

'No need, you can give me another under the mistletoe ball later. Now shall I carve the goose?'

Lily hoped the roast goose was cooked to perfection and was pleased to find the meat with onions and the vegetables she served with it were delicious. When she looked round the table she thought how lucky she was to have a wonderful family to share the day with.

'I'm sorry I haven't put coins in the plum pudding.'

'We don't need them. I don't think we need the pudding either,' Samuel added, patting his stomach appreciatively.

'You'll have to have some as it's been steaming for a couple of hours. It would be a pity not to at least try it.'

After the meal they took the children upstairs for a nap and then sat by the fire in the parlour.

'What would you like to do, Lily? Sing, play the piano, read?'

Lily wouldn't have minded a nap like the children, but wanted to make the most of her time with Samuel. 'Why don't you read to me?'

'Do you know A Christmas Carol by Charles Dickens?'

'No, I don't,' Lily said.

'I know Eta and Mabel have some works by Dickens. Let me look through the bookcase and see if I can find it. I'll read some of it and we can finish it on other days.'

Lily made herself comfortable. She had trouble keeping her eyes open although she found the story interesting.

Eventually she fell asleep and was woken some time later by a loud banging at the front door. Lily had no idea who it could be, but she must answer it before the noise woke the children.

She glanced across at Samuel and saw he was just waking up, too. It must be one of the neighbours.

As she pulled open the heavy wooden door, she recoiled and tried to shut it on her visitor, but it was impossible to match his strength.

# 18

Cecil stepped into the hall shaking his fists, his face florid. 'I've come for my children. Where are they?' he shouted. Lily froze. This couldn't be happening. He was dead, wasn't he?

'I'll have a drink first.' He staggered into the parlour and slumped into one of the armchairs. Lily followed him, her legs shaking.

Samuel was on his feet, anger filling his face. 'Get out of this house,' he shouted.

'What? Get out of the house my children own? You talk too much, Samuel. You've been chatting to your landlady, Cora, about my late wife's will and how the twins inherited the house. You gossip, Samuel, and the gossip has spread. Now how about that drink?'

'I'll get it,' Lily said.

If they could calm him down by doing what he said maybe he would see reason. Her heart thumped as she thought of him taking the children. They were such happy, carefree children, she couldn't bear to think of their lives with this vile man.

'Here you are, Cecil.' Lily put a glass of sloe gin next to him. He drained it in one swift gulp.

'I expect the children are upstairs,' he said, heaving himself out of the chair and heading for the door.

Lily exchanged a worried glance with Samuel. 'I won't let you have the children. They are loved, safe and happy with us. You were never fond of them. How could you?'

Lily could feel actual rage building up inside her. She loved those children and she knew now that she would do everything in her power to keep Sylvan and Archie safe.

'Whatever you might think of me, maid, I am a good businessman.' Cecil winked at her. 'I have already engaged a woman to look after the dear children. After Mabel took a swipe at me and left me bleeding, I was lucky that a caring woman I had got to know took pity on me and invited me into her house to look after me. We will move into The Limes together. Oh, don't look so surprised.' He started staggering up the stairs. 'I'm going to see my precious children.'

As Cecil reached the top of the stairs, with Samuel following him closely, there was a rap at the front door. Cecil appeared not to have heard it, but Lily was hoping for someone to help.

She ran and opened the door to a beaming Reverand Harold Mason.

She beckoned him inside and he started to explain he had come to thank her for her thoughtful Christmas gift, but after looking at her he said, 'Are you all right, Lily? I can tell you're not. What is it?'

'Wait here,' said Lily as she took the stairs two at a time.

As she reached the top of the stairs, Cecil was shouting at Samuel.

'You'll leave my house at once!' he spat.

'It's not your house. Mabel left it to

Lily and the children,' Samuel told him.

Cecil's face turned red and bulged with anger. Just as Lily had reached the pair, Cecil reached forward and pushed Lily who plunged backwards and bounced down the stairs.

As she lay in a heap at the bottom of the stairs every part of her aching, she became aware of Reverend Mason leaning over her in concern and talking to her gently, asking if she was all right. 'Please go and help Samuel,' she begged.

When she awoke, Lily was lying in bed with Samuel beside her, holding her hand.

'How do you feel?' he asked.

'Where are the twins? Has he got them?' She tried to get up, but Samuel gently held her in his arms.

'It's all right, Lily, they are safe. Cora is looking after them downstairs.'

'Where are Cecil and Reverend Mason?' Lily couldn't bear to hear that Cecil was still in the house.

Samuel smiled and stroked Lily's hair.

'Harold is great — almost super-human. Who would have believed that a man of the cloth could fight like that? He helped me hold Cecil down and kept him under control while I ran for help.'

'And where is Cecil now?'

'The police took him into custody and Harold went along as he was a witness.'

'A witness to what?' She nudged Samuel, 'Get on with it.'

'He was a witness to Cecil pushing you down the stairs.'

# 19

Lily had heard that brides felt nervous on their wedding day, but she didn't have one shred of anxiety. All she wanted was to be with Samuel for ever. She'd hated the time they'd spent apart and now she could declare her love for him in the sight of God and their union would be blessed by Reverend Mason.

He was a good man and she valued their friendship. Cora had very kindly offered to look after the children. They would be at the wedding, but Lily needn't worry if they started crying or making a fuss. Cora was a capable and loving woman. She had also been helpful in arranging the food for the wedding breakfast and had enlisted the help of Ada and Mrs Cousins.

Lily wondered what Eta and Mabel would have made of things. She decided to walk to the churchyard and pay her respects to the sisters and their parents.

It would have been wonderful if her own mother could have been at the wedding, but she'd have to write and tell her all about it and perhaps Samuel would paint a picture of the two of them in their wedding finery.

The early morning dew seeped into her shoes and she wished she'd worn a sturdier pair. Lily remembered the January morning two years previously when she'd trudged through the snow to The Limes not knowing what was in front of her. It had been an adventure. Thoughts of Cecil Potts entered her mind and she quickly dismissed him. She wouldn't let him ruin her special day. Shivering her way to the grave, she bent her head in prayer and then hurried back to the house.

'Lily!' Lily heard the shout and thought she was dreaming as she caught sight of her mother in the parlour with Cora and the children. She blinked hard and then ran into her mother's outstretched arms. At that moment, there was no need for words as love flowed between the two of them as they clutched each other.

Then her mother said, 'You didn't think I could miss your wedding day, did you? Samuel arranged for me to come. Cora has been telling me what a lovely mother you're being to the little children. They're behaving very well.'

At that, Archie banged his pull along toy into the wall and seemed to enjoy the noise it made, so he did it again. Not to be outdone, Sylvan did the same with her pig. Cora tried to stop them, but they were enjoying themselves too much to take any notice of her.

Lily bent down and scooped up the twins. 'This is my mum,' she said.

Sylvan put out a hand towards her and Mrs Harrison took it. Peace was restored.

'Shall I take the children?' asked Cora, coming forward. 'I expect you will want to let your mother see your wedding dress.' She spoke to Mrs Harrison. 'My friends will be over soon to get the food ready.'

'Can I help with that? I have brought

a few things with me.'

'That's all right, Mrs Harrison, you spend your time with Lily.'

'Please call me Maisie.' Mrs Harrison smiled at Cora before Lily pulled her upstairs to help her get ready.

'It was very thoughtful of Samuel to help me be here. I can't thank him enough. You are lucky to have found someone like him.'

'And he is lucky as well, Mum,' teased Lily, hugging her.

'Of course he is. I hope you'll be happy like your father and I are. He sends his love and I must tell you about your brother Claude's new job.' The two of them chatted as Lily put on her pink wedding dress and arranged her hair, asking her mother's opinion every now and then as she listened to the news from home.

When she was ready she stood in front of the mirror and her mum stood next to her looking at her reflection. 'You look beautiful,' she said, dabbing her eyes with a handkerchief.

Lily couldn't wait to walk to the church to meet Samuel. Maisie, Cora and the children walked with her on the short journey, and the sun made a shy appearance. Clutching a posy of delicate white Queen Anne's lace, she left her companions at the church door and caught a glimpse of Samuel's head near the altar. Her heart lifted and she almost raced along the aisle to meet him. He turned, smiled his sweet smile and held out his hand to her.

The ceremony passed in a blur of words and promises and when Samuel slid the wedding ring on her finger, Lily almost fainted with happiness. Samuel held her hand and they left the church to return to The Limes.

The wedding breakfast was nowhere near as extravagant as Mabel's had been, but there was a good selection of food. It was heartening to see Cora, Ada and Mrs Cousins laying food on the table in the dining room, but Lily found she had no appetite. Love had taken it away.

'I love you, Mrs Parker,' whispered

Samuel, his breath tickling her ear. 'But I shall have to be the polite host and talk to people when I'd rather just be with you.'

Lily nodded. 'I'll look after Archie and Sylvan and talk to Mother. It is such a lovely surprise to have her here.'

'Lily,' called Ada, 'you must have something to eat. A slice of pork pie? I made it myself.'

How could she refuse? 'Thank you, Ada, it looks delicious.' She accepted the plate and walked over to her mother.

'There's lots of food, Lily. I expect your father and brothers will be sorry they weren't here when I get home and tell them all about it.'

'You must take some back for them. And thank you for the chicken you brought and the blancmange. It makes a pretty centrepiece.'

Maisie laughed. 'I didn't think I'd get it here in one piece. I know it's a favourite of yours, but I thought it would end up in a mess.'

It was wonderful to have a homely,

easy conversation with her mother and Lily wished she could stay with them for at least a week. Sadly, she would be going home later in the afternoon.

Archie and Sylvan were getting restless, despite the attention they were given. 'I'll get some of their toys,' said Lily, 'but if I leave the children on the floor they might get trodden on.'

'We can't have that,' said Maisie, taking charge. 'Shall I take them upstairs? I can play with them.'

'I'm supposed to be looking after them,' said Cora, coming over to them. 'I'm sorry, Lily, but I don't seem to be doing a good job.'

'Of course you are,' said Lily. 'It's a bit chaotic in here, that's all. You're trying to help everyone.'

'Perhaps you'd come up with me, then,' said Maisie. 'Bring some food and we can have a little party of our own.'

Cora smiled. 'I'd like that. You go on with the children and I'll follow you.'

Lily was pleased that her mother was fitting in with her friends. Perhaps she'd visit again.

The wedding cake was a Victoria sandwich made by Lily the previous day. She hadn't wanted a grand cake. It looked attractive covered in sieved sugar and she'd wrapped ribbons around it. She looked around the room, all in all, it was a very acceptable spread of food.

'What have you done with the twins? Sold them into slavery?' asked Samuel, touching her on the arm.

'That's right. I hoped you wouldn't find out.'

'Time to cut the cake?' he asked.

'Let's give it a few minutes, shall we? I must tell you something important. Can we slip into the scullery on our own, do you think?' Ignoring Samuel's puzzled frown, Lily led the way.'

Samuel shut the door of the scullery behind them. 'What is it? What's wrong?'

'I just couldn't wait any longer to tell you how much I love you, Samuel.' She placed her arms around his neck, pulled him to her and kissed him long and passionately.

Finally the kiss ended, but they still clung to each other. 'We will have a long and very happy life,' Samuel assured her. 'Nothing will come between us.'

Alone at last in the bedroom, Lily was sitting on the bed, patted it and said, 'Come and sit next to me. Tell me you enjoyed our wedding day.'

Samuel sat next to her and took her hand. 'It was the happiest day of my life, so far. The beginning of January may not be the best time for a wedding, but I thought it perfect. I was blessed to be marrying the most beautiful bride on earth and when it snowed as we left the church I found it enchanting.'

'And you'd arranged for my mum to be there. That was special for me.'

'She got on well with Cora and the other village women. I'm sure she will try and visit again. I am sorry it wasn't possible for your father and brothers to be here too, but they had to work and it would have been an extra expense.'

Lily snuggled into Samuel, inhaling the clean smell of his skin. She let out a contented sigh. It had been a glorious day and she didn't want it to end.

'It was kind of the women in the village to lay on the wedding breakfast. I'm very happy they now think of me as their friend and see me as respectable.'

'A married woman, no less!' Samuel put his arms around her and Lily fell into his embrace.

When they broke apart, Lily stood and looked in the mirror.

Samuel came up behind her, placed his hands on her hips and kissed her neck. 'You look beautiful and I think Mabel would be pleased you wore her wedding dress. You are extremely clever to have altered it to fit you.'

She turned to face him. 'And I think you are extremely clever choosing me to be your wife. Mabel and Eta would have been pleased I was married in the same church where Mabel was married although maybe it doesn't bode well.'

There he was again. Cecil. Always at the back of her mind ready to ruin anything good.

'Don't think of that, Lily. Our marriage will be solid, unlike Mabel's. We aren't going to take advantage of each other or be cruel. Our home with the children will be happy and filled with laughter. The biggest difference between us and Mabel and Cecil is that we love each other.'

'You are right, Samuel,' said Lily, 'Now can we please not talk of Cecil Potts again — at least not tonight.'

Samuel put his hands on her shoulders. 'May I unpin your hair?'

She nodded and he gently took out the decorative combs.

'Your hair looked beautiful. When I was at the altar and turned to look at you I felt a wonderful sense of completion and peace. It may have been a small wedding, but it was perfect. Just like you.'

'It was wonderful.' Lily felt as though she would burst with happiness.

'Now we have pleased the gossips, Mrs Parker, let's make the most of each other!'

# 20

Lily could hardly contain her excitement, but she would have to wait for Samuel's return to tell him all the good news. As she hung the washing on the line in the garden she sang and did little dances making the children, who were playing under the love tree, smile. After hanging the last garment she walked over to join them.

Sitting with her back against the solid trunk she took in the perfect scene of spring. She thought all the shades of green must be there and the yellow daffodils were adding a touch of brightness.

The children were playing happily with their pull along toys and, as she watched them, her happiness overflowed. Everything was going well. If Samuel came back with news that he'd found a cottage for them, then her joy would be boundless. No, she reminded herself, there was still some strange news she had to tell him.

In an attempt to put that out of her mind she pictured the cottage, with higgledy-piggledy rooms, low beams and sloping floors. A garden with hollyhocks, foxgloves, lupins, delphiniums, and fragrant roses round the door. She had put her trust in Samuel to choose their new home well, but he had been away too long and she was missing him. Every day she longed for it to be the day of his return.

Back in the kitchen, she made bread dough and gave the children a piece each to play with on the floor. Sylvan broke a piece off to put in her mouth and thought it a good game when Lily said no. Repeating the action and causing Lily's reaction made her laugh. As Lily kneaded the dough on the table the game continued. Previously, she hadn't needed to make bread as village women had supplied it to be sold in the shop.

The sound of the back door opening had them all looking to see who was arriving. Lily's heart pounded when she saw it was Samuel and she threw herself into his arms, not caring that she was covering his clothes in flour.

'My darling,' he said, before kissing her fervently. 'How are you?'

'We are all far happier now you are back. It seemed such a long time that you were away. Do you have good news? Did you find us a cottage, a home?'

'I did, but I am tired and hungry. I started my journey very early this morning because I couldn't bear to wait any longer before I saw you all again.' He walked over to the children and picked up each in turn to kiss and tickle them. They squealed with delight.

Lily made tea and put food on the table. 'Samuel, come and sit with me and eat.'

She made the most of the quiet time as Samuel ate, to study his features. He looked thinner and tired, but still had the same twinkle in his eye when he glanced at her.

When he had finished, he reached across and took her hand.

'I have found a delightful cottage for us to live in. The village is small, but the people I met were friendly and welcoming. The cottage has three small bedrooms, one for us, one for the children and a spare one. Downstairs there is a parlour and a kitchen and scullery. And the garden! You should see it. In summer it will be a riot of colour. There is just one failing to our new home.'

'Oh, Samuel, is it something dreadful?'

'It doesn't have a love tree.'

She sighed with relief. 'That doesn't matter because it sounds as though you have found the cottage I have been dreaming of. And I have good news for you too. We had a visit from a man who works for a big brewery. He was looking for properties to set up public houses and had heard that The Limes is for sale. I showed him round and he liked it and said there and then that they would buy it.'

'That's wonderful news, Lily!'

She smiled. 'I have some other wonderful news. You mentioned a spare room at the cottage. We will need it, for we are going to have a child.'

Samuel leapt from his chair, pulled her up into his arms and swung her round, hugging and kissing her.

'My happiness is complete!'

Lily revelled in his joy, then said, 'I have something more to tell you, which will make you cross . . .' They both sat down again. She didn't want to spoil the mood, but she would keep no secrets from the man she loved. 'A policeman visited us.'

'What? Why?'

'The policeman said that he thinks Cecil will be charged with more crimes. Incriminating evidence was found at his lodgings.'

'What sort of evidence, Lily?'

She frowned. 'I don't understand how a father could think of doing such terrible things to his children, Samuel. There was some paperwork about a penny life insurance for the twins. He could only have benefitted from that if they were dead.'

Lily's hand flew to her mouth. She

could barely get the words out. Her voice shook as she said, 'He said that some fly papers were found there as well. And a newspaper cutting about arsenic poisoning.' Lily grabbed his arm. 'Don't you remember telling me the story of the two sisters who killed by using arsenic? I can hardly believe that anyone would kill their own children, but in Cecil's case, Samuel, I do.'

Lily looked out of the window of the brougham at The Limes. She had mixed feelings about the house. It had been a place of unkindness and unhappiness, but also a place of unimaginable joy. 'I'm ready for a new life. The five of us in the cottage you say is idyllic.'

Although she thought Samuel would have chosen the perfect home for them, she would have liked to have seen it before moving in. It hadn't been practically possible for her to visit the cottage, as it would have been an extra expense and upheaval with the twins. There were some things which she would want from a home which perhaps Samuel wouldn't even consider to be important. However, because she hadn't seen it, she was very excited at the prospect, with a quiver of unease at what she would find.

Archie wriggled in her lap, wanting to get down on the floor.

'Look, Archie, there's Aunt Cora, Auntie Ada and Mrs Cousins. And everyone else. They've all turned out to wave to us.'

It felt rather bold setting off in a brougham and she'd baulked at the cost. 'Our neighbours will think we are grand when we arrive in our new village.'

'I wanted you to have a comfortable journey. And it's easier with the children. Wave, Sylvan, look, all our friends. There's Harold Mason too. Everyone who stood by us.'

'I am sad to leave them, but now I think it is best for the children to move away from their past. We will tell them about their father, of course, when they are old enough to understand.'

She kissed the top of Archie's head and wished they would have memories of their loving mother, but they were too young.

As they left the village Lily sighed and relaxed back against the seat.

'It's an adventure. I hope we have packed enough of our possessions. We seem to have very little.'

'We are renting the cottage and there is already enough furniture.'

'Where is the cottage? Are you ready to tell me your secret?'

'Wait and see. I am sure you will be pleased by its location.'

After all the activity of packing, Lily felt tired, but her excitement kept her awake on the journey and it grew when she recognised places they passed through. 'This looks familiar.'

Samuel grinned at her.

Not long afterwards she sat forward in her seat. 'My goodness, I can't believe where we are. This is my village. Where I grew up and where my family live. Oh, Samuel, you've brought me home!' Tears formed in her eyes.

When they pulled up outside the cottage, which she remembered well and was the one she now realised had been in her imagination, she burst into tears.

'I'm sorry, Lily, I thought you would be happy.

We don't have to stay here. I am sure we can find somewhere else to live.' He looked distraught as he passed her the handkerchief she had embroidered for him.

'I am crying for happiness. I am the happiest woman alive. Thank you!'

The cottage was just as she remembered when she'd passed it when she was younger. A gate between hedges led to the wooden front door which was surrounded by pale pink climbing roses. She paused on the doorstep to breathe in their fragrance. Having never been inside the cottage before she was eager to explore. In the kitchen the table was laid with cakes and supplies.

'Your mum has left those for us. She said you must see her as soon as you are settled.'

There wasn't much furniture in the cosy parlour so it left plenty of space for the children to play. The kitchen and scullery weren't as large as at The Limes, but she could get used to that and it meant there would be less cleaning to do.

When she unlatched the door at the bottom of the stairs and went up to see the bedrooms, she was happy to see a sun-filled room for herself and Samuel, with a large bed on which was laid a colourful patchwork cover.

Across the landing was a sizeable room with two little beds which would be just right for the twins. Against one wall was a roomy cupboard which should house their clothes and toys.

She held her breath as she opened the third door and peeped in. Her hand automatically went across her stomach and she was delirious with happiness. She loved the twins to distraction, but a little baby made by herself and Samuel was an added blessing. Her mother would be very pleased to hear the news that she was to be a grandmother. The room was tiny, but it was big enough for a little cot and a chair. There was no need to worry about where her mother might sleep as she lived close enough to easily return home after visiting.

When she went back downstairs, their possessions were unloaded and piled in the kitchen. The children were in their high chairs each enjoying a piece of gingerbread.

'I've put the kettle on. We'll have some tea and cake and then maybe you'll tell me where you want things to go.' Samuel held a chair out for her at the kitchen table and served her with tea.

'Tea,' sighed Lily, sinking into the chair. 'Thank you, Samuel. You look after me — us — very well.' She reached for his hand and put it to her lips.

'Are you pleased with the cottage?'

'I love it. I've had a good look around and I think I can work out where I would like things.' Lily sipped her drink and thought of their future together. Could things be all right with a fresh start in a new village? Or would the memories of Cecil Potts follow them?

Lily soon developed a routine at Rose

Cottage and loved the place. Samuel and she adapted to a different way of life, with Samuel going out exploring, sometimes taking his painting equipment and sometimes his notebook. The twins seemed happy and played together with their toys just as they had at The Limes.

The neighbours were nice people, some of whom she'd grown up knowing. They spoke to her and the children when they were in the garden.

Lily often went outside to hang out washing or tend the garden and would find the time had flown by as she chatted about the weather and the various goings on. Sometimes they exchanged recipes and had get togethers at each other's houses. It was a free and easy time for Lily and her pregnancy continued uneventfully.

'Here, Sylvan,' she said one day. 'Take this.' She formed the child's hand so the food for the chickens would sit in it, then she guided it towards the pecking hen. The children giggled even when being pecked. Nothing seemed to upset them for long. It had been Samuel's idea for them to have chickens. 'We all love eggs,' he'd said, 'and your roast chicken is the best I've ever eaten.'

Each day, Lily, Sylvan and Archie collected the eggs, although Archie was a little less keen on doing it after he'd squeezed one so tightly it had broken. His little chin had quivered and Lily had gathered him up, saying it didn't matter. He'd clung to her and sobbed into her neck.

'We're going to make a cake today,' she said, one day. 'You two have been very helpful gathering the eggs and we're going to make one of your mother's recipes. She was an excellent cook.' Lily thought it important to remind them of Mabel's part in their lives.

She enlisted as much help as she could from the children and they all sat waiting for the cake to be cooked and cooled.

'Oh, you know when to come home, don't you?' laughed Lily as she laid out a pot of tea and some milk for the children.

'Cake!' said Samuel, kissing the three of them. 'What more could I ask for?' He sat down and tickled the twins before reaching for Lily. 'I've missed you,' he said.

'I think your stomach brought you home, don't you, children?'

Archie banged the table with his hands and Sylvan reached for her milk.

'This is one of Mabel's cake recipes,' explained Lily. 'I'd like to save a piece for Mum's next visit.' It was good that she was able to be a frequent visitor to Rose Cottage. Lily was relaxing and enjoying her new home and surroundings.

There was a knock at the cottage door one morning when Samuel wasn't at home. Lily expected to open it to a neighbour. She was surprised to see Reverend Mason standing there. Why was he visiting her?

'Good morning, Lily.'

'Please come inside,' Lily said.

Lily's heart thudded and she felt faint. She sensed he had come with bad news.

He ducked his head and followed her

into the cottage. 'It's about Cecil Potts.'

She'd felt all along that they'd never rid themselves of that man. She was pleased to see Reverend Mason, but wished he was there for a different reason.

'Sit down and I'll get you some tea. I think you are tired and worried. What a long way for you to come and visit us.'

'It was a long journey, but one I felt I should make, given the circumstances.' He slumped onto a chair and Lily went to the kitchen.

When she returned, Reverend Mason sat up straight and smoothed a hand over his hair.

'It's quite serious, Lily. I had a message to visit Cecil and I felt it my duty to do so. He's been taken to hospital and is in a bad way. I think it's probably pneumonia or bronchitis that he has. I stayed with him all last night. He could have been delirious, but he was adamant that I was to see you and ask you, Samuel and the children to visit him. He is allowed visitors if I accompany them.'

'Why?' Lily asked. 'What does he want

with us?' In her heart, she didn't want the children anywhere near Cecil Potts and a hospital was no place for them.

Harold Mason raised his shoulders, 'I have no idea. But would you see him? I would come with you. I think it's important, Lily. He's dying, I'm sure of it.'

'I don't want to see him in the slightest, but if you think I should, then I'll think about it. But now you must rest. You can lie on our bed.'

'I could sleep on the clothes' line.' He smiled wearily, and followed her up the stairs.

About an hour later, Samuel arrived home and Lily quickly told him what had happened.

'Well, I'm not going to see that man, he's evil. And you're not to, either. And I forbid the children to see him.'

'Don't tell me what to do.' Lily was upset. Samuel had never spoken to her like that before. 'I'll decide what I do. And what the children do.'

Harold Mason appeared in the doorway.

'Hello, Samuel. Lily's told you the news, I expect.' He sat on the edge of a chair and stared out of the window. 'It's not an easy decision, I know.'

'Huh, it's very easy for me, the answer is no. I will not see Cecil Potts!'

'I'd better be on my way, then. I was hoping I could accompany you, but I see your mind is made up.'

'It is.'

Lily packed some food for the Reverend and walked to the main road with him.

'I'm sorry, I wonder if I should go, because I trust your judgement, but it will be difficult to persuade Samuel. I will write to you to arrange a visit if we decide to see Cecil.'

Harold Mason smiled. 'It's good to see you again, Lily. What a beautiful cottage you have. And, am I right, you are expecting a baby soon?'

Lily nodded. 'We have been very happy living here. And my mum lives a short distance away. We can see each other whenever we want to.'

'I'm pleased. I always had a soft spot for you. You're a kind and gracious woman, Lily Parker. God bless you.'

'I hope he will. Have a safe journey.'

Lily walked as slowly as she could back to the cottage. She didn't want to argue with Samuel, but his mind had seemed to be made up that he would not visit Cecil.

Samuel was in the kitchen giving the children some milk and a biscuit.

'I've made some tea,' he said, as he poured it into cups. 'Please sit down and let us discuss this quietly.'

Lily did as he asked.

'I absolutely will not let the children visit that man.' He sat in the chair next to her and took her hand.

'I won't either, Samuel, we are agreed on that.'

Samuel pulled his hand away. 'So you still think you might visit him? Why when he has caused the people we love pain?'

'Because he is dying and wants to see us. He may be sorry and want us to forgive him.'

'I will never forgive him. He is a cruel man.'

'I agree.'

'Good, that's settled.' Samuel was about to stand up. But Lily put her hand on his arm.

'No, it is not. I think I should visit him. I will visit him whatever you say.'

Samuel left the room without another word.

Lily didn't ask for help with her writing when she got in touch with Reverend Mason and the atmosphere in the cottage was tense.

'Lily, I am worried about you going to see that Mr Potts on your own.'

'I'll be fine, Mum, but thank you for visiting before I set off.' Lily picked up her bag and kissed her mum. 'Reverend Mason has agreed to meet me and he will accompany me. I shall be quite safe.'

'I shall be with her as well.' The two women turned and looked at Samuel who was ready in clean clothes. 'Is that all right, Lily?'

'Oh, Samuel, it's more than all right.

I shall be much happier if you are with me.'

Maisie made a discreet retreat to the garden after saying she would care for the children until they returned. Lily and Samuel hugged each other.

When they walked into the ward and to Cecil's bedside, Lily could see immediately he was in a bad way. His breathing was laboured and his cheeks sunken.

Reverend Mason spoke first. 'Cecil, Lily and Samuel are here to see you.'

Cecil opened his eyes and a slight smile creased his face. 'So you've come.'

'What is it you want to say to us?' Samuel asked firmly.

Lily had to lean forward to hear the words. Cecil's voice was faint and rasping. 'I want you to know what I did. You think you got the better of me, but I killed Eta.'

Lily grasped Samuel's arm. 'What do you mean?' she asked Cecil.

'Arsenic. I was the one who made her sick and caused her death,' he replied.

'But why would you do that? She was a

kind woman and never did you any harm.'
Lily glanced at Samuel. 'Why would
he?' Then she realised, if Eta was dead,
Cecil would be able to take advantage of
everything Mabel inherited. She wanted
to hear more from Cecil. 'Are you sorry?'

'Sorry? No, I'm glad.' He closed his
eyes and turned away.

Samuel led Lily out of the ward.

Reverend Mason followed them,
looking flustered. 'I am very sorry. If
I'd had any idea why he wanted to see
you I wouldn't have asked you to come.
I thought maybe he wanted to make
amends for some of his actions before
he meets his maker.'

'He hasn't changed at all. Samuel,
let's go home.'

Having had a fitful night's sleep, Lily
found herself wanting some fresh air, so
after giving the children a light meal, she
took them out in their pushchair. The
countryside was beautiful and she sang
to the children as she pushed them along
the country roads.

She stopped by a field and, as Archie

was content, took Sylvan out of the pushchair and pointed out the things she could see. Lily smiled as the child snuggled closely to her. Archie struggled to be free and with his sister. For a brief moment, Lily wondered if she might have twins. Heavens above! All those mouths to feed. What would Samuel think? He would probably be delighted as he seemed to be a natural father. Thinking of him, she decided to return to the cottage and await his arrival.

She'd just settled the children with a drink when she heard the back door open. 'Samuel, we're in the parlour. Come and have some tea.'

'Hello all of you. I finished painting the scene I was working on and decided to come home to see you. I like it best when we're all together.'

'So do we, dear Samuel,' smiled Lily.

As Samuel drank his tea, he asked, 'And what have you been up to today?'

'We've just come home from a walk to the fields. I was thinking about seeing Cecil. I am pleased you changed your

285

mind and came with me. It made it easier for me, but I know you didn't want to see him.'

'I had to be with you, Lily. I wanted to protect you, keep you safe, even though Cecil was in hospital and you had Harold Mason with you. I couldn't bear the thought of you facing that wretch without me by your side. I love you so much.'

Lily couldn't believe the gem she had found in her husband. 'It was a gesture of love and I thank you, dear Samuel. I wish we didn't know what Cecil did. It's hard to think about.'

'It is tragic that he killed Eta, but it will be easier with time to forget him. I'm glad you wanted to visit him and I'm glad I decided against my foolish idea not to go with you. It was the right thing to do. You are a good person, Lily. Your influence makes me a much better person than I would be without you.'

Later that evening, with the children tucked up in their beds, Lily and Samuel sat in the parlour. Samuel brought out his notebook and started writing and

Lily reached for her work basket. She still enjoyed sewing and had brought some material with her from The Limes with which to make clothes for the new baby and also for the twins. She glanced across at Samuel and saw the familiar smile on his face. He always looked happy since their move to Rose Cottage. Their eyes met and the look he gave her was so tender it melted her heart.

'Are you all right, Lily?' he asked, putting down his pen and coming over to her chair. 'You don't have to work so hard. You'll soon have four of us to run around after.'

'I will, will I?' asked Lily, raising an eyebrow at him. 'What happened to that bit when you said you'd look after me?'

'I love you very much.' Samuel knelt on the floor at her feet and put his arms around her. 'You're getting really big now, aren't you?'

'Did anyone tell you that you're a charmer?' She suddenly leant forward and cried out.

'Lily, I'm sorry, I didn't mean to upset

you. Please forgive me.' Samuel was on his feet and cradling Lily awkwardly in his arms.

'It's the baby,' gasped Lily. 'I'm sure it is.'

'What should I do? How can I help? Tell me, Lily.

Shall I get your mother or one of the neighbours?' He edged towards the door, brushing his hands through his hair.

'Calm down,' Lily managed to say as the pain ceased. 'Just get the midwife.'

Up in their bedroom at Rose Cottage, Lily and Samuel became the proud parents of a baby girl. It had been a relatively easy and straightforward birth. Lily was tired, but didn't want to sleep. She held Myrtle to her breast and basked in the love of Samuel whose gaze was fixed on his little daughter. Tears glinted in his eyes and Lily had never felt as close to him before. Is that how love was? It carried on getting better and stronger every day, with problems, adversities, setbacks and magical moments. She believed it was.

# 21

Lily stood at the back door of the cottage enjoying the sun warming her body and the sounds of the twins, now nearly two and a half, playing in the garden. Samuel had taken Myrtle out in the pram earlier and was now sitting on a stool in front of his easel, the pram by his side with Myrtle sleeping peacefully.

As promised by Samuel, the garden was ablaze with colour. Foxgloves and roses vied for space. Bees busily visited the blooms seeking out nectar, and birds sang in the hedges. It was idyllic and Lily couldn't have been happier.

She wandered over to her favourite rose bush and, gently taking one of the flowers with its delicate velvet petals in her hand, she breathed in the heady fragrance. Then she stood as still as she could to watch butterflies dancing.

Slowly she made her way to stand behind her husband. Putting an arm on his shoulder she leant over to study the watercolour he was working on. It was a painting of the cottage and garden, bright and vibrant. 'It's beautiful, Samuel. It captures the soul of this heavenly place. The colours are brighter than your usual work which seems to have a softer, dreamier quality.'

'You sound like an art critic! This one is for us, if you'd like it in the cottage. As you know, my other less vivid paintings are selling well now and I enjoy working on them. This one is for you.'

'I'd love to have it in the cottage. I'm not sure whether it would look best in our bedroom or in the parlour. Rose Cottage has style now, due to your pictures.' She sat on the grass next to him.

'My pleasure. I would do anything for your happiness.' Samuel set aside his paint brush and sat beside her on the grass before leaning over to kiss her cheek.

Lily spotted another painting on the ground beside the stool. 'What's this?' Reaching for it, she was puzzled as it was torn in two but she thought she knew why. It was a dull painting, in greys and browns. 'It's The Limes!'

Samuel rested his head on her shoulder. 'Yes, it is. I painted it when I was at my lowest ebb there. At a time when nothing was as it should be, except my love for you. That was the only thing which kept me going.'

'It was only because you were there that I was able to live in the same house as Cecil and do my best for Mabel, Eta and the children.'

Lily knew it would have been very difficult for her to remain at The Limes if Samuel hadn't been there. The three women had relied on him for his strength, kindness and wisdom.

'We are blessed to have found true love, Samuel. Look at our children.' She looked at Sylvan and Archie who were busy collecting and putting stones in an old bucket and tipping them out again. Then looked at their baby. 'You were clever to think of a fitting name for our youngest daughter. Myrtle, the tree of victory. Together we have overcome all the difficulties we had to face and now we are victorious. Her name reminds me of those joyful times we spent under the love tree in the garden of The Limes. But our happy future is here, not there.'

'But it wasn't all bad, it's where we met after all. I love you, Lily.'

'I love you too,' said Lily. 'And I always will.'

*Other titles in the*
*Linford Romance Library:*

# A BODY IN THE CHAPEL

## Philippa Carey

Ipswich, 1919: On her way to teach Sunday School, Margaret Preston finds a badly injured man unconscious at the chapel gate. She and her widowed father, Reverend Preston, take him in and call the doctor. When the stranger regains consciousness, he tells them he has lost his memory, not knowing who he is or how he came to be there. As he and Margaret grow closer, their fondness for one another increases. But she is already being courted by another man . . .

# BLETCHLEY SECRETS

## Dawn Knox

1940: A cold upbringing with parents who unfairly blame her for a family tragedy has robbed Jess of all self-worth and confidence. Escaping to join the WAAF, she's stationed at RAF Holsmere, until a seemingly unimportant competition leads to her recruitment into the secret world of code-breaking at Bletchley Park. Love, however, eludes her: the men she chooses are totally unsuitable — until she meets Daniel. But there is so much which separates them. Can they ever find happiness together?

# THE LOMBARDI EMERALDS

## Margaret Mounsdon

Who is Auguste Lombardi, and why has May's mother been invited to his eightieth birthday party? As her mother is halfway to Australia, and May is resting between acting roles, she attends in her place. To celebrate the occasion, she wears the earrings her mother gave her for her birthday — only to discover that they are not costume jewellery, but genuine emeralds, and part of the famous missing Lombardi collection . . .

# TURPIN'S APPRENTICE

## Sarah Swatridge

England, 1761. Charity Bell is the daughter of an inn keeper. Her two elder sisters are only interested in marrying well, whereas feisty Charity is determined to discover who the culprit is behind the most recent highwayman ambush. And by catching the highwayman, she aims to persuade Sir John to bring his family, and his wealth, to her village. It may also make the handsome Moses notice her!

# REVENGE OF THE SPANISH PRINCESS

## Linda Tyler

Cornwall, 1695. When her beloved father dies with the name Lovett on his lips, privateer captain Catherina Trelawny vows revenge on the mysterious pirate. Seeking him on the Mediterranean island of Azul, she is charmed by the personable Henry Darley. But Cate finds her plan goes awry when Darley and Lovett turn out to be the same man. Cate and Henry set sail across the high seas battling terrifying storms, deadly shipwreck, dissolute corsairs — and each other.